THE BATTLE WITHIN

THE GHOSTS OF REDRISE HOUSE

CAROLINE CLARK

SPOOKY NIGHT BOOKS

THE GHOSTS OF REDRISE HOUSE

This is a three book series that that tells the story of the spirit. Old Hag. Each book can be read alone but I think you will enjoy them more if you read them in order.

Book 1: <u>The Ghosts of RedRise House – The Sacrifice</u> 0.99 for a limited time only and FREE on Kindle Unlimited.

Book 2: The Ghosts of RedRise House – The Battle Inside

Book 3 The Ghosts of RedRise House – Beware the Children.

* * *

<u>The Ghosts of RedRise House Book 1 - The Sacrifice</u>

Rosie is running from her past. Looking for peace and a new beginning. House sitting in the luxurious and romantic RedRise House seemed like a perfect plan to rediscover herself and rebuild her life.

It is so far away from the past that she knows she can look to

THE GHOSTS OF REDRISE HOUSE

the future and yet something is not quite right. She hears voices, footsteps in the night. She wakes from terrible nightmares. Strange figures stare down at her bed with hidden faces--was it all just a dream?

Then there are the ghostly children. Are they all part of her imagination or did something terrible happen here?

Like animals, the children fight for her blood. Will they get it or is something darker waiting and watching for its chance to escape?

Find out if Rosie will ever leave RedRise house or if she will join the children to stay in this haunted house for all time. The Ghosts of RedRise House – The Sacrifice Just 0.99 for a limited time and FREE on Kindle Unlimited.

* * *

**Get a FREE short story and never miss a book. Subscribe to Caroline Clark's newsletter for new release announcements and occasional free content:
http://eepurl.com/cGdNvX**

PROLOGUE

RedRise House
Yorkshire Moors

England.

THE BATTLE RAGED inside Rosie's mind. Time and again she fought for control against the darkness that slithered, cold and demanding. Matron, the evil within, was like a snake curling around her mind and controlling her. Like smoke she seeped into the deepest recesses and filled her thoughts with despair.

Fear ruled her almost as much as the spirit. Sometimes she would gain control and get to her feet but before she made it to the door, her limbs would go weak and she would drop to the floor. There she would lie, convulsing as the battle between them raged. Eventually she would lose, and a feeling of cold, dark despondency took over. It was like the deepest depression she had ever known, and Matron loved it. The smile that pulled her lips into a grimace displayed the woman's joy.

Whenever Matron took full control she would talk at her, gloating and exulting in her new found power.

"You are mine now," her voice hissed inside Rosie's mind. "You have no free will, no control. I will find all those you love and I will make you watch as I tear them apart. Then they will worship me. They will add to my power and you will be nothing but my puppet."

No! Rosie screamed in her mind but her voice was fading. It was getting harder to talk, to think, and she could no longer control any of her limbs.

Inside her mind she beat against the walls of her own brain, beat against the evil that held her trapped. It was exhausting, and many times she wanted to curl into a metaphoric corner and give in. Only she couldn't. She wouldn't give in on the only real friend she had.

Amy.

That one thought kept her going, kept her fighting. No matter what, she would save her friend.

For two days she fought for control but she was getting weaker. Matron was winning, and as her anger subsided, fear took its place.

During that time they sat in the corner, in the dark. She hadn't eaten, drank, or slept, and she was tired, hungry, and exhausted. Now this morning, Matron forced her to move. Stiff-legged, she walked her to the bedroom and there she began to prepare.

Rosie knew she had to do something. The images Matron

THE BATTLE WITHIN

flashed within her own mind were terrifying. She would not allow the spirit to use her to kill others; she would die first. That thought was like a light bulb going on in the darkness. She nurtured it, hid it, and allowed it to give her hope.

Hour after hour she kept the thought away from Matron, looking for the perfect time. Gradually she was dressed and her clothes were packed, along with a few books and what looked like a silver pentagram necklace and a black cloth. Rosie tried to gain control of Matron's thoughts, tried to find out what they meant, but she couldn't. Then she pulled out a knife. It was made of a bright silver metal. The wickedly curved blade was as thick as her hand at the hilt and curved down to a sharp point.

The leather of the handle felt moist against her fingers. It was once the purest skin cut from the untainted white belly of a day-old calf. Years of use had darkened the leather. It looked black, but if she squeezed it tightly enough, it would release the blood of all her victims.

There was no time for that now. She turned the blade. It glinted in the light as if winking at her. Giving it a smile and a nod of gratitude, she buried the sacrificial knife in and amongst her clothes.

The last thing that was packed was the book. It was one she had found in the basement, the one about the life of this house. It was called, *The Sacrifices of RedRise House and the Resurrection of Old Hag*.

A groan escaped Rosie and she was surprised that her body, her captor, allowed it. Maybe she had a little control left. Carefully, she hid her joy by expressing even a little of the fear she felt.

The book was shoved on top of her clothes and her own

hand stroked lovingly across the cover before closing the bag, careful, so that the cover was not damaged.

Rosie knew the book was written by various people who had been part of Matron's story. The first was Bartholomew Matthews, the man who had unwittingly unleashed her onto the world. He had a daughter named Mabel, a sickly child who was dying. One night, in a fit of despair, he had asked for help. The spirit that answered him was not kindly, not of this world, and desperate for escape. It got what it wanted, taking the soul of his daughter in exchange for saving her life.

Matron was thinking about the book, about her own story and how far she had come. She was so happy with herself and so secure in her hold over Rosie that she let her guard down.

On the dresser, Rosie spotted a pair of nail scissors. They were small, but sharp and would puncture her jugular if she acted quickly enough. Gradually she let go of the fight, let go of control of her body. As she did, she felt a smugness within. Matron was proud and powerful; she wasn't used to dissension.

The spirit thought she was weakening, that she was giving in. Trying hard to hide her thoughts, she concentrated on her legs and right arm. The dresser was just two feet away.

She knew all Matron wanted to do now was leave this place. She would let her think that she had won.

As Matron used her body to pull her top over her head, Rosie waited. Once the top was clear, she stepped to the side and reached down. Her fingers clasped onto the scissors. They were small and cold. She was so close now. Her intention was to slam the scissors into her own throat. She waited,

THE BATTLE WITHIN

relaxed, and then moved with all the speed she could muster. Hoping that the surprise attack would be over before Matron could understand what she was doing.

The world slowed down and her hand arched through the air, the silver scissors gripped tightly in her sweaty palms. As they traveled toward her neck, she thought about Amy and tears ran down her cheeks.

It was a strange thought, taking place in a fraction of a second.

The scissors raced toward her throat, whistling as they rushed through the air. Just as they touched her skin her hand stopped.

The scissors pressed against the skin. All she had to do was move her hand a few centimeters and it would be over. If she did it fast enough she could pierce her own jugular vein and she would bleed out here in RedRise House. She would die, but Matron would once again be trapped and her friend would no longer be in danger.

Sweat coursed down her back as she willed her hand to move.

It was like pushing against a battleship. No matter how hard she tried, her hand wasn't going anywhere. In her mind she gritted her teeth and pushed with all she had. The fight was exhausting. Her arms bulged and sweat broke out and ran down her face, but nothing happened.

Panting, she relaxed for a moment and waited for that little smugness to return inside of her. Once it was there, she tried again.

The scissors rushed a few millimeters closer, indenting the skin, but her hand was stopped once more. The scissors were pushing into the delicate skin of her neck, but never piercing, never drawing blood. Just a little bit more and she would perforate the flesh, but it was not to be.

A vicious pain sliced through her head. It was as if the scissors had been plunged deep into her brain. As if they were open there and cutting into her cerebral cortex.

No! She screamed inside her head, but her lips never moved. She had no control over them, and then she felt her arm move and the pressure against her throat was gone.

Still she strained against the invisible force that held her arm which stopped her from ending this.

No, you are mine and I am your master, the words commanded inside her head. *You will do as I say. You are mine for all eternity.*

A vision of Amy slashed to pieces filled her mind and Rosie screamed, "No!" She would never give in and she swore that she would never hurt anyone. Though her own life may be over, she would do everything she could to stop this creature from killing again. She would do everything she could to end its life.

Her fingers opened and the scissors fell to the floor with a small clatter. Against her will, her foot kicked them away and an evil laugh curled around her brain.

Get out of me! She screamed in her head, but she was answered with another laugh.

Her body turned and faced the dresser, staring at the mirror. She knew the person reflected back was her as she bore the same scar across her left cheek. The same brown eyes and the same long brown hair. She knew if she looked at the skin on her right forearm that there would be burn marks. Despite all of this, she didn't recognize the person in front of her. The eyes were malignant and cruel. The face pulled down into an expression that reflected superiority and dominance. There was no warmth and no hope.

Rosie knew the mistake she had made and that there was very little she could have done to prevent it. When she ran from her past life; when she took the job house sitting in this remote haunted property, her fate was already sealed. The house had been occupied for many years by the evil spirit, by Matron, her acolytes, and the poor suffering children.

It had been brought to this property by a desperate father, a man who simply wanted to save his daughter. Now that spirit, that entity, wanted out and Rosie was to be its transport host. All she could do was sit within her own mind and scream out her protest.

* * *

It was two days after she was possessed that Rosie's best friend Amy arrived. Rosie was tired and weak and had almost given in. Matron had changed her clothes but she had not showered and she knew that she smelt of stale sweat. Would Amy notice? Would she say anything?

Her friend would never mention it, though hopefully, she would think it strange. Maybe she could use that. Maybe she could trick Matron into doing things that would give her away. It was all she had, and she kept the thought deep inside.

"How are you doing?" Amy asked, as she bounded into the house, her dirty blonde hair stuck up at all angles and yet, as always, looking perfect. With a big smile she pulled Rosie into a hug.

Matron shrank back, disgusted at the contact, amazed at Amy's scruffy, albeit fashionable look.

It gave Rosie a chance and her mouth opened. *Run, get out of here*, formed in her mind and she could have sworn that she spoke the words as Matron pulled away from Amy.

"You look tired. How's it going?" Amy asked, her eyes drawn down with concern.

You have to run, to get away from me, Rosie tried to say, but this time she knew her lips hadn't moved.

A smile curled onto her face while she was screaming, shouting and pounding on the inside of her skull. Anything to make Amy see the danger before her, only none of it could be seen.

"I am. This just didn't work and I want to leave," Matron said. "I contacted the owners and they say it's fine. I'm just to lock up and post the key."

"Don't you want to hear the good news?" Amy asked, as her pink lips gave that cute little smile that said she was teasing.

Matron was impatient. "No, can it wait?"

"Hey, Rosie, what is it?"

Rosie felt Matron crawling through her memories, like so many worms crawling through her brain, and she tried to shut them down. Tried to make it hard for the spirit to learn from her, but it was no use.

"Sorry, I've just been having nightmares. About Clive. I think he may have found me," Matron said with Rosie's voice while in the darkness of her mind Rosie screamed.

Amy laughed and pulled her into another hug.

THE BATTLE WITHIN

Matron squirmed inside and Rosie was sure that Amy would feel the way she was backing off. Her friend had to know her well enough to know that something was wrong.

Amy pulled back and smiled her big goofy smile. "That's just it. He's been arrested. They found him trying to get back into your old place and he's in jail. You're finally free."

Inside her prison, Rosie started to cry. That was great news and yet she would never be free... not ever again."

"That is such good news. Now let's go celebrate. I could kill for a decent... Mocha." Matron stumbled on the word 'Mocha' as she didn't know what it was. Could Rosie use this? Could she use the fact that this spirit, this thing, had been trapped here for decades, perhaps centuries? It wasn't much, but it was a start.

"You and me both," Amy said. "But before we do, I bought you something to celebrate. I knew you had been looking at it and I wanted you to have it... kinda a new beginning gift. Here."

Amy handed over a black velvet bag.

Matron held the bag in her hand and searched through Rosie's memories. She was trying to find the right thing to say but Rosie fought against her. It was no use. "Thank you so much. I know what it is."

"Then open it, quick!" Amy was back to her old excited self. Her brown eyes sparkled with joy.

Matron opened the drawstring bag and tipped it into her hand. Out came a silver necklace with a pink crystal rose. Her eyes widened and her lips pulled back from her teeth. For a moment she almost flung the cheap costume jewelry back at Amy, but at the last moment she stopped herself.

Even without Rosie's cooperation she knew that was the wrong response.

Biting her lip, she looked up at the strange woman. "Thank you for being so kind," she said stiffly.

Amy pulled her into her arms and hugged her tightly. When she pulled away she took the necklace and placed it around Rosie's neck. Matron wanted to push her away, wanted to rip the cheap thing off her neck and hurl it to the floor. Instead, she forced a smile on her face.

*　*　*

Soon they were in Amy's car and as she drove away, Rosie looked back at the house. What was currently beautiful fell strangely and rapidly into a state of disrepair. The garden filled with weeds. Tiles were gone from the roof and the windows were broken. The front door was hanging off the hinges and the place looked as if it had been abandoned for decades. Maybe it had; maybe it was only Matron keeping the place alive.

Surrounding the door were a dozen or more children and two adults hidden in hooded cloaks. Rosie remembered them. Each child had been sacrificed to Matron. They were her power while she was at the house. Rosie had managed to free a few, but Matron had taken her over before she could release them all. As they moved away from the children would Matron weaken? Logically, she thought that she would, and she searched her mind trying to gain access to Matron's thoughts as she had gained access to hers.

No, the word was hard in her mind and followed by pain as she let out a yelp.

"Are you okay?" Amy asked.

"No," Rosie managed to say. *Leave me here, I'm possessed*, she said in her mind but 'no' was all that passed her lips. "I just have a headache," Matron completed the response for her.

"Oh, I'm so sorry. I thought this would be really good for you."

Rosie had lost control, at least for now. She turned to look at the children as they drove slowly away.

The two adults stood at either side of the door, like sad statues destined to crumble and fade into nothing. The children were different. They tried to follow, but each time they got more than twenty feet from the entrance, they would disappear and snap back to the front of the house. It looked like they would be trapped there forever.

I will release you one day, Rosie said in her mind.

"No, you won't," a cold voice replied. "You will stay here and watch me murder your best friend. Then you will help me gather souls to become strong and powerful. You will watch me slaughter throughout the centuries and you will hate it. That hatred, that fear, will make my control all the more delicious."

Rosie screamed and shouted and raged at the prison that was her mind, but the only response she got was a deep and evil chuckle. She had lost and the world would pay for her foolishness.

CHAPTER 1

atigue dragged Rosie down, forcing her into the seat and willing her eyes to close. The world was like treacle, like mud. With every movement she was fighting against a force greater than she was. She had to rest.

So she let go and tried to rebuild her thoughts. She knew there were areas of her mind that Matron couldn't reach. Places where she could hide. Places where she could plan. She imagined a vault in which she kept her deepest thoughts. That was her place. Somewhere Matron wasn't allowed. It was somewhere she could go to hide and to think. If she was going to keep Amy alive.... she had to do something.

As the car drove away, the warmth and the motion lulled her into a sense of peace and security. It was false, but it was all she had for now.

Matron was picking at her thoughts, trying to decide whether to kill Amy now or whether they needed her for the moment.

Rosie relaxed, placing her real thoughts inside the vault; she imagined being afraid of driving. It wasn't hard. Clive, used to shout at her when she drove. All she had to do was cultivate those feelings of fear and insecurity.

As they surfaced, a red rage dropped behind her eyes. Matron was angry. She wanted Amy dead and she wanted it now.Inside her vault Rosie smiled. It looked like Matron needed to kill. Like she needed to sacrifice Amy to gain her soul. Rosie thought back to RedRise house and all the children that Matron had sacrificed there. All the souls she had gathered. Maybe without those souls she was weaker.

"You're very quiet," Amy said.

In her mind Rosie cultivated anger at her friend for interfering. For asking about her life and for not leaving her alone. If she could push Amy away then it would keep her safe. Maybe her friend could even help her, if she acted strangely enough.

"Why shouldn't I be quiet," Matron said.

"Sorry. Rosie, are you all right?"

"I don't see what you mean. Of course I'm all right. I just don't need to be bothered by your inane questions. Now, if you will let me rest, I will let you know when I need something."

Rosie could feel that Matron was happy with the look that crossed Amy's face. Her own emotions were mixed. Amy was hurt and confused. It was a start. Though she hated to upset her friend, more than anything she wanted to upset her. Wanted to drive her away, far away, to safety.

The journey continued in silence. To Rosie it was murder, a living hell, and she knew it would be the same for her friend. From time to time Amy glanced across at her. The deep furrows in her brow showed that she was concerned. Rosie wondered how she could use this. How she could get her friend to safety or maybe she could get Amy to help her.

How long is this journey? Matron asked in her mind.

Rosie didn't want to answer; she didn't want to give this woman, this creature anything, not even that, so she stayed in her vault.

Pain lanced through her brain and she let out a yelp.

"Rosie, what is it?" Amy pulled the car over to the side of the road.

As the car stopped, Rosie was released from the pain, she was panting heavily inside, and fighting for control against the agony, but outside she breathed normally.

They were out in the countryside, somewhere she didn't recognize.

How long until we get to somewhere that I can kill this woman? Matron demanded in her mind.

Rosie fought with all she had, shaking and pushing against the force that held her thoughts so tightly. It was excruciatingly painful. Like needles inserted into her brain and yet she could tell that she had a stupid grin on her face.

The pain increased and she screamed in her own mind. Did it matter if she gave in on such a small point? Somehow she thought it did. She believed that every time she gave in it would become easier the next time. Or if not easier to give in, then harder to resist.

I don't know!" she shouted at Matron. *I've only traveled this way once and I don't remember.*

Matron bristled inside her mind. Angry that she couldn't get what she wanted. It was a small victory, but Rosie was going to enjoy every one she got.

A series of images flashed through her mind: They were in a cellar. It was dark. A flame flickered from a torch on the wall casting shadows around her. A feeling of weakness and yet euphoria overtook her. A heavy robe hung on her shoulders. It smelled of sweat and a coppery substance that she knew was blood.

To her side stood a taller figure. Cloaked in the same garb, she couldn't see his face. In front of them was a stone platform, an altar and a young girl was held upon it. Four cloaked figures surrounded her. One on each limb, but she was no longer fighting, but simply lying there knowing what was to come.

She was desperately thin, her eyes wide and afraid and yet there was a resignation in her features... as if she had always known that this was coming... as if it was all she could hope for.

Rosie wanted to run to her, wanted to hold her in her arms and tell her that everything would be all right. She wanted to take her away from there. True enough, she was advancing toward the girl, but the thoughts in her mind were no longer on rescue. Terror, pain, and damnation swirled around her brain and she was exultant to be inflicting it on the young girl.

Together, step by step with the man on her right, she approached the terrified girl. Shadows cast across her shoulders. They splayed on the wall like gargoyles creeping up on her. Each time the shadow crossed her face, the girl shied away. Trying to sink into the stone and slink away from the terrors.

Rosie felt her right arm rise above her head and she looked up to see a wickedly curved blade. It wasn't held in her own hand but in one gnarled and twisted with swollen arthritic joints.

Euphoria ran through her at the same time as a sick dread. The part of her that was Matron was reliving one of her favorite memories. Taunting Rosie with what was to come. The knife plunged down, dragging her arm with it. Rosie's mouth opened and she let out a sigh of ecstasy as the knife struck flesh and sliced deep inside the girl.

Her arm was jolted as the knife tore through flesh and hit the stone bench below. Warm blood ran over her hand and the part of her that was still Rosie reeled in terror. That part of her that was now Matron was strengthened by the vision. It glanced across at Amy and a sick smile spread across its face.

Rosie gasped for breath as the vision cleared. What was she to do? What had she unleashed on the world and how could she stop it?

You can't, a voice said in her head. *I have been waiting for someone just like you for so long. I selected well. I will ensure that you and all those you love shall suffer.*

CHAPTER 2

*R*esignation, along with horror, fear, and sickness washed over Rosie, but for now her fight was gone. Exhaustion finally got the better of her. It was too hard to fight, too painful, so with tears that she could not shed, she let go and slunk back into her vault. There she would recover and plan.

As she retreated into her vault, a coldness filled her, chilling her to the bone as Matron smiled. She knew that she needed to regain her strength and she just prayed that Amy would survive until she could.

Rosie was still vaguely aware of her surroundings. It was like floating just above a drug-induced sleep. Much like she had felt after having her wisdom tooth removed. The world was there; it was just fuzzy and dark, a little out of focus, and the conversation was just out of range of her hearing. For now she would have to let Matron take control, knowing that at least during the journey, the spirit couldn't kill her friend.

"I'm really worried about you," Amy said.

THE BATTLE WITHIN

"Why?" Matron snapped.

"Because you're so different. I found you that job; was it really so bad?"

Silence filled the car and Amy shuffled in her sear.

"Rosie, I'm so sorry if I made things worse for you... I never wanted to... I thought it would be good for you."

"Do you not understand boundaries? I don't want to talk about it," Matron snapped, and Rosie could feel her searching for information, for answers on how to react.

Rosie kept her mind as still, as silent as she could, and did nothing as Matron picked and picked at her brains. It was working. She had kept her thoughts inside her vault and for now Matron did not understand. Maybe she thought that she was exhausted, but with a long sigh, she backed off.

"Maybe we could get that... Mocha?" Matron asked. "I feel the need for one."

"Okay, but don't you want to shower first?" Amy asked.

"Shower? Oh, that; I only bathe on Friday... what day is it?"

Any was looking out of the window but her eyes were pulled down and her mouth had dropped open. She turned to Matron and raised a perfectly trimmed eyebrow. Asking if this was for real, when she got no answer, she drove on a little way in silence. Soon they turned onto a motorway.

Matron gasped at the sight of so much traffic. She had seen the occasional car. Every time she lured someone to the house they would arrive in a vehicle, and over the centuries things had changed but here now—it was overwhelming.

For a moment, fear tugged at her and she regretted the

decision of leaving her home. Of leaving behind her souls. Out here in this noisy, dirty world she was vulnerable. She had to kill and she found herself staring at Amy's neck. Maybe she could just kill her here and now. It would give her strength, but her knife was in the case in the back of the car. There was another problem.

Pulling her eyes from the sweet skin, pulsing with blood, she licked her lips and looked out of the windscreen. The world rushed toward her at a dizzying speed and everything was so foreign.

How she wanted a drink. Sweet, warm blood would be her choice, but she would settle for water, wine, or tea. Anything to ease the dryness of her throat… and what was a Mocha?

Rosie had given in. The girl was weak and feeble. Right now Matron was pleased. She didn't feel strong enough to fight but it caused her a problem. If Rosie let her mind collapse then she couldn't use her for information. The world had changed so much, she was going to need that source of knowledge. Apart from that, it would have been fun to torture her. How she had enjoyed the torment she had given over the years. Firstly to the young girl, Mabel, whose soul had been her doorway into this realm.

A laugh escaped her as she remembered how the scared and sickly girl had still fought. Like a little tiger she had thrashed, spit, and scratched to be free, but it was all to no avail.

Amy was looking across the car, a strange expression on her face.

Now what?

"Is something wrong?" Matron asked trying to keep her tone as conversational as she could.

"I wondered what was so funny."

Amy was staring back out at the roaring vehicles as they overtook some huge metal monster. Matron gripped onto the seat and put a hand to her chest. Her heart was pounding so hard she could feel it against her palm. This could not be good but what could she say?

Again she searched around the remnants of Rosie's mind for an answer but nothing was there. She wanted to blurt out that she was reminiscing about torturing Mabel and then how delicious it was to see her father, Bartholomew, come to terms with the fact that he needed to kill his own daughter. Those had been her glory days and she would have them again. Then an answer came to her.

"It was just something from my book. I did quite a bit of writing and... well you know me and the characters."

"I'm so glad you were able to write. Did you get the book finished?"

Oh why won't she shut up and let me rest? "My book will never be finished," Matron said, and in her mind she could see the book that she had brought with her. *The Sacrifices of RedRise House and the Resurrection of Old Hag,* only that wasn't what Amy meant. It was the silly romance that Rosie had been writing.

"I thought you had a deadline?" Amy asked.

"Yes... that book... it's nearly finished. I just meant, that as an author, one's work is never done."

"I see that," Amy said, and then she turned the car off the road and down a narrow lane.

Matron knew that she was failing, that she was making too

many mistakes and that Amy would become suspicious. The woman had to go and she had to go soon.

Now she was driving too fast down a narrow path with a concrete wall too close, too close. Matron let out a yelp.

"Hey, it wasn't that close," Amy said as she pulled the car into the services. There was a Costa Coffee sign up ahead and she parked near the entrance.

Matron stared at all the cars lined up. What were they doing here? Was it some kind of market?

Amy grabbed her bag and got out of the car. Matron stared after her and waited but Amy simply started to turn away. Matron sat waiting for Amy to open her door. It didn't happen, Amy was just looking at her. She rummaged in her mind, causing a spike of pain where she thought Rosie was. She could feel the remnants of Rosie and knew that she was expected to follow Amy for the mysterious Mocha. Only she didn't know how to open the door and then she looked down as she had no idea how to get out of the car. For a moment, panic squirreled in her mind and she started to scrabble at the door until she found the handle.

When she found it, Matron was filled with relief but Rosie could feel fresh sweat running down her back. This was taking it out on the spirit, so maybe she could use that to her advantage. Quickly she shut down and retreated into her vault.

"Come on slow coach!" Amy shouted. She was waiting on the pavement which was flooded with people.

Matron wanted to stop and stare. So many people, so many souls for her to take, to control. It was too much and so was the noise. There was traffic everywhere. Great big monsters that lurched toward her and the sound of the traffic was a roar in her ears. It was all so tiring. She wanted to rest, to recuperate, and to rejuvenate for she knew that she was aging. If she didn't kill soon then this body would fail her. Once again, her eyes were drawn to Amy's neck as she looked at the car. Could she get the knife, maybe find somewhere quiet and kill this woman?

Then what?

Maybe she could kill a few people here and gain control.

A thought came into her mind, you would be caught and killed first. Was that Rosie? Was she playing her?

Matron wondered if the girl was maybe not as weak as she thought. Maybe she was clever and sly. It didn't matter; she would bide her time and she would have her soul. So she followed Amy, but while she did, she filled her mind with the image of a knife slicing into Amy's throat. Inside her mind Rosie recoiled and she had her answer. Rosie was cleverer than she looked.

CHAPTER 3

Matron followed Amy into the services and knew that her mouth was open. So many people and they all looked so different. She knew about different clothes but this was just overwhelming. The room buzzed with noise and there was so much bright light that she just wanted to curl into a corner and hide.

"Are you all right?" Amy asked as she passed her a tray.

Matron looked at the plastic item that had been smeared with a damp cloth and she wanted to drop it.

"I'm fine, well as well as I can be here," she spread her arm to indicate the room.

"I know you hate these places but I'm hungry and thirsty. We won't be long and you will be home in an hour or two."

"Really, that's the best news I've had in a while."

"You look a little shaky, why don't you take a seat and I'll get us both something?"

Matron smiled and nodded but where would she sit? Then she saw a quiet corner and made her way over. Once there she closed her eyes and rested. This was so much more exhausting than she'd imagined. It had taken years of planning to make this escape and now it was all failing because she couldn't kill Amy. Anger flooded her and she knew that her face was red. Clenching her fist tightly, she dug her nails into her palms until they drew blood. It centered her and she opened her hands and licked away the red fluid.

It tasted of life, of strength and it was a start, but she needed more.

Amy put a tray down on the table with bacon and eggs which she pushed across to Matron as well as a large mug with what looked like hot chocolate. Her own food was some orange colored sauce and Matron felt her eyes widen.

"I know, I always eat curry but this looks really good," Amy said as she tucked into her food.

So that was curry; it didn't smell like real food. Matron ate her bacon and sipped at the drink. It was very sweet and very strong and she couldn't stomach it.

"Tell me what's wrong?" Amy tilted her head and smiled sweetly.

Matron knew she had to do something to stop the woman's suspicions so she searched Rosie's mind once more. Picking away until she found something to use but it was exhausting. "I'm just so tired. The house was so lonely and every noise I heard I thought it was Clive. Then when you come and tell me he's been caught... I guess it's all just too much. I have this terrible headache and I just want to sleep for a week."

"I'm sorry. Well you have your place back now and you can go home. Get some rest and I will come see you in a day or two. Okay?"

"All right, that would be nice."

Soon they were back in the car.

"Do you mind if I sleep?" Matron asked.

"No, you go ahead. I'll wake you when we get there."

Matron closed her eyes and searched Rosie's mind. Slowly she went through every nook and cranny she could find for she knew that Rosie was hiding. It was exhausting work and would take her a long time, but she would find the girl and she would root her out. Then she would have total control.

With her eyes closed and sweat running down her face she searched and probed, but it was all to no avail. Rosie had hidden well.

"We're back," Amy called and reached over and shook her friend.

Matron started out of her search and opened her eyes. She was weak, rundown and struggling to stay awake. Yet she must for if she lost consciousness then Rosie may regain control.

"Are you okay? You're soaked in sweat," Amy asked.

"Maybe I have an infection," Matron said. "A few days' rest and I'll be as good as new. If not, you can send for the physician for me."

"What?"

"I just need a little bed rest and maybe a leech or two." Matron gave her best smile.

"Good joke, but I think we'll just get you inside and into bed. I have some paracetamol which will help with the fever. Come on."

Amy helped her out of the car and into a small residence. It was neat and tidy, if a little sparse inside. Amy left her staring around while she fetched in the case and placed it on the table.

Matron gasped as her hand went to the zip.

"Leave that!"

"What?"

Matron was so exhausted it was hard to hold on. She was losing control and if this stupid woman didn't go soon she feared she would. Then what?

"Let me help you unpack," Amy said.

"I will unpack later right now I just need to lie down..." She hadn't meant to say that and she tried to walk to the case to grab the knife, for now that she was here she could kill Amy.

"No!" Matron didn't know whether she had shouted the word or whether it was just in her mind. Amy was staring at her but didn't look too bad. It must have been in her mind.

Again she tried to walk to the case, but her legs wouldn't move. She felt her mouth opening and couldn't stop the words that came out.

"You have done so much for me but can you leave me for a few days?"

Amy nodded and came over and pulled her into her arms.

Matron bristled at the hug, but the body she was in relaxed into it and she felt tears prickling at her eyes. *She will die,"* she said in Rosie's mind. *Today or another day, it doesn't matter... she has to die.*

No, I won't let you, I will die first, Rosie managed in her mind. "Then she pushed Amy away a little more aggressively than she intended.

"Rosie what is it?"

"I don't want you catching whatever I've got. I'll ring you when I'm better. Now please, just go."

Amy nodded, her face creased into a frown, but she turned and left.

As soon as the door closed, Matron and Rosie battled inside. It was like a hurricane inside Rosie's head, one of pain and fear and desolation. Before she realized it, she dropped to the floor and lay on the wooden boards, convulsing and shaking. Image after awful image was forced into her brain and she felt the pain and fear of all of Matron's victims. The children that she had left at the house had been sacrificed every few years. Each one adding to the powers of the beast, and she knew that Matron was desperate to kill again. The only thing stopping her was Rosie. So she had to be strong, had to stay in control, but bit by bit, she was weakening.

Again and again Matron lashed at her mind, but there was another thought. Amy was safe. At least for now. Maybe it was time to rest.

That one thought gradually took over and Rosie let go of the pain and the exhaustion, falling into a deep sleep. After all, while she was asleep what could Matron do?

CHAPTER 4

2 2 Clay Pit Lane,
Leeds,

Yorkshire,

England.

MATRON REGAINED control lying on the cheap wooden floor. It wasn't even hardwood, just made up of badly varnished floorboards with a worn rug thrown to one side. The harsh light above her was like a needle in her brain but none of that mattered. What mattered was that she was weak, so very weak, and she needed souls to make her whole again.

She hauled herself to her feet and from the window could see that it was already dark outside. That was good. It was always easier to hunt in the darkness and yet she was afraid of leaving the house.

Maybe she should just stay there until Rosie awoke?

Such a thought shocked her; it must be the remnants of Rosie's mind and she must be careful. *This one was tricky.*

Standing in the cold room she could feel her clothes were damp with sweat. The shirt stuck to her back and armpits, but that also didn't matter. A wave of dizziness and pain in her stomach drove her to the sofa. There she clung onto to the faded pink material until it passed.

This was not good; she must hurry. On the sofa was her case. It called to her and she staggered around and sat down beside it. With a shaky hand she reached for the zip but it was hard to grip. Looking down she saw Rosie's hand. The woman was almost thirty and yet the hand changed before her eyes. The smooth skin wrinkled. The elegant fingers contorted. The joints swelling and twisting and then the worst happened: Matron was wracked with a painful lung wrenching cough.

The frail hand raised to cover her mouth as she endured the attack. Each cough tore through her lungs and chest and filled her body with fever. *The consumption was back.*

A sense of despair pushed her down like the weight of all her victims. Leaning back against the sofa she closed her eyes and bit down on her lip. "No!" The word tore out of her and echoed around the room. She must not give in. This was to be expected.

Again she coughed, closing her eyes, she let it come not giving in, but knowing better than to fight death itself. She could trick him, slow him down, but to fight would be a pointless waste of energy that she didn't have.

As quickly as it started the attack passed, but it left her exhausted, and when she drew her hand away it was once more the delicate hand of Rosie, only it was covered with blood.

Mabel, the child she originally possessed, had died of Consumption. That thought took her to her happy place as she remembered Bartholomew's desperation. His need to save his daughter. It had been her salvation, her entry into this world, but nothing was without consequences. Every ten to twenty years she needed to take a soul to heal her body of the disease, to restore her. Without it, this body would die and she would return to the hell that she had so desperately escaped from. That was not an option. She had to find souls, to restore her body and to boost her strength. Then she would have some fun.

She drew in a tentative breath. If the consumption still had control, then it would be like breathing in needles. The air found its way into her lungs and there was no pain, just a little tightness. She had time—but she must hurry.

Unzipping the bag she saw her book there. Delicately, she lifted it out and placed it on the sofa. She would need to update it soon. A lot had happened since she last wrote an entry that she had a plan to escape.

Beneath the book was her knife. The thought of the blade increased her pulse and drove away the last vestiges of fever. As she clasped the handle, the leather felt warm and moist in her palm. It filled her with strength and she knew she was ready. She could do this and soon she would have all the power she needed. Soon she would heal this body and build up a collection of souls. Then she would be invincible and Rosie would simply be her plaything.

With a new spring in her step she walked to the door, pulling it open and stepping through. Just before she closed it, she remembered the keys that Amy had used to get in. Picking them up, she grabbed a jacket from a rack near the door and slipped the keys into a pocket.

Taking a deep breath, she stepped out into the street.

A cold wind stuck the shirt to her body and chilled her to the bone. The knife was in her right hand and she tucked it inside the jacket. The wind made the handle feel so cold, not soothingly warm like the blood that had stained it.

She had to be quick, to find someone to kill before she didn't have the strength.

Turning to the right, she began to walk. The street lamps gave some light, but there were long shadows between them. It was ideal, but there were very few people that she could see. This may take time and she was already growing weak.

A car went past and the lights lit up a couple across the road. Matron licked her lips and felt her throat ache for the taste of blood. They were walking hand in hand and laughing as they looked at each other. They would be perfect, but they were too much for her tonight. She would have to find one person alone, preferably a young or old person.

CHAPTER 5

Walking past the couple, Matron pulled the coat around her. As the cold air hit her chest and was pulled into her lungs, the urge to cough was overwhelming. Swallowing, she fought it down. Now was not the time to succumb to the wasting disease. Now was the time to stalk, hunt, and to sacrifice.

And yet the empty streets mocked her. For what seemed like forever, she walked down dark and dreary streets. They were all the same and so confusing. The houses set in little crescents which were too open for her liking. From time to time she heard the sound of footsteps or laughter. Occasionally she saw a curtain twitch as she went past, but she never found the right person.

Everyone she saw was strong or in a group, and that was no good. No good at all. Then she came to the edge of the estate and the houses changed. The street lights were further apart. The houses rundown. The gardens full of debris, and there were dark passages and alleyways for her to hide in.

Finally, a cough escaped her and she bent double as it wracked her body. Rosie was a nicely shaped woman with meat on her bones and yet when the cough hit, Matron felt thin and frail. It was as if she was shaking her very core and she feared something would tear lose or break. She had to stop thinking that way; the cure was close at hand and in these new surroundings, these new hunting grounds, maybe her luck was changing.

Then she saw what she needed. An old woman was struggling down the street with a heavy bag. Matron crossed the road and fell into step behind her. For a moment the woman turned around. The flare of a cigarette lit up a wizened and tired face surrounded by long gray hair that drooped over her shoulders. There was fear in her eyes but it relaxed when she saw Rosie.

Matron gave her a smile.

The woman pulled her threadbare pink jacket around her shoulders and walked on so slowly that Matron had to slow her own pace and shorten her stride. It was too cold to be walking so slovenly but she didn't want to rush this. She had to wait for the right time.

So she followed and cursed inside. Step by step her body failed and still the woman walked on. Struggling with her shopping and occasionally puffing on the cigarette. Matron hoped that soon this gift would turn down somewhere quiet, somewhere lonely enough for her to make her strike.

The woman tossed her cigarette down and it flared as it hit the ground. Matron had the urge to rush over and stamp it out but she hung back, for it seemed that at last luck was shining on her. The woman turned up a narrow alleyway with no street lights.

Matron's breath caught in her throat, only this time it wasn't the consumption but excitement that held it there.

As she reached the entrance to the alley, she paused. Should she follow straight away? If she did, would she risk her prey becoming scared? Would the old coot flee?

The thought was amusing. The alleyway was long, narrow and dark. There was nowhere to run. In this new younger body she could easily chase her down and complete her sacrifice, and yet she felt so weak—could she?

Turning up the alleyway she began to walk slowly and carefully, placing her feet with precision so as to make not a sound.

The woman passed out of sight and a burst of adrenaline had her heart pounding and her breath coming too fast. She rushed forward, only to hear the creak and groan of a rickety old wooden gate being opened.

This would not do. How dare this bitch escape her!

Forcing her aching and exhausted body into a trot, she covered the darkness as quickly as she could. Luckily for her she had always had good night vision. The rough and broken tarmac gave her feet no problem, and as she rounded a bend she saw a gate closing onto the alleyway.

The woman had gone.

Sprinting forward she reached for the gate and forced the knife into the gap just before it closed. Grinding to a halt she gasped for breath as the old woman slammed the gate once more.

"What the devil is wrong with this thing," a frail voice

gravelly from too many cigarettes, came from behind the fence.

Matron felt a flush of victory and knew that her prize was close. The gate was made of old boards. At about six foot tall it guarded the secrets behind it but it looked tired and old. Ready to give in and let the devil pass.

Matron kicked at the bottom board. The gate sprang back and a loud yelp brought a smile to Matron's face.

The gate was shoved back and Matron kicked it again. This time a board came free and the gate flew open.

The woman bent over holding her nose as hot red blood poured out and ran through her fingers.

Matron could almost taste it, the coppery sweetness on the air, and her throat ached.

The knife was hot in her hand and she raised it above her head. This wouldn't be the perfect sacrifice but it would do.

The woman's eyes widened so much that they were like dinner plates in her face with just tiny dots of brown sauce in the middle. Just like some posh meal, Matron thought

Matron began her downward swing facing east. In her mind she imagined a bright blue light, the color of Satan, entering her finger and charging her body. In her mind she sent praise to Lucifer.

The knife arched through the air and down toward the woman's neck. The idea was that she would slice from the left side, at a 45-degree angle. It would sever the carotid artery and she would drink the blood while completing her ritual. Without helpers, it was the best, quickest, and safest way.

Euphoria was already hers as she imagined the energy she would take from this woman's spirit. Then she would harness her soul and force her to power her existence for all eternity. It was a delicious moment, less than a heartbeat away, but with her adrenaline pumping so fast time seemed to slow down so much that she could be moving through treacle.

Just before the knife hit its point, the woman stepped back and at the same time she kicked out with her right leg.

The blow contacted with Matron's left kneecap and forced it back knocking her off her feet.

A scream was ripped from Matron and she dropped the blade as she fell to the floor.

Anger surged through her and she screamed out her frustration, "Damn you!"

The pain sliced through her knee and ripped up into her groin. Tears came to her eyes and she felt an awakening inside her head. *No!* She shouted to herself. *No, you will not take over*!

Only it was too late. The pain freed Rosie from her prison and she could see through her eyes once more, could move her body, and as she looked out she saw the fear on the old woman's face.

What was happening?

CHAPTER 6

Shock, fear, confusion, and pain hit Rosie like a herd of bulls. They collided with her mind and bowled her off her feet. She was falling backward as her knee gave way and she jumped with it in an attempt to escape the world in which she found herself.

Matron cursed in her head, swearing and tearing at her mind. Determined to regain control, and Rosie knew she wanted something, needed something.

What can it be?

As they hit the ground, a pain ripped through her coccyx and rose up into her skull. For a moment she was stunned and so was her passenger. She wanted to shut down to get away from there, but she sensed that she must fight for control. That maybe she even had a chance. There was something different about the presence that had hold of her mind. It felt smaller, weaker, and less overwhelming.

Before Matron could move, she got to her feet and looked around.

An old woman was standing there, holding her nose and looking at them with wild eyes. On the floor near her feet was a huge, shiny knife. Rosie didn't remember having it and yet she knew it must belong to Matron. The wickedly curved blade glinted in the moonlight and yet the handle was dark. Looking at it sent a shiver down her spine, as she remembered it from her dreams back at RedRise House. Back where this all began. Where this spirit forced its way inside her; where she lost her life.

For a second she thought about grabbing the knife to keep it away from Matron. Only that was ridiculous. Once she had it, if the Old Hag took control again, then she already had the knife.

"Run," Rosie shouted at the woman. "Run and get away from here."

Slowly the woman let go of her nose. The bleeding had stopped but her face was smeared with blood and tears. Her hands were shaking and she looked as if she would start to cry, but not as if she could move.

Rosie turned back to the fence. Maybe her best bet was to get as far away from here as she could. Grabbing hold of the gate, she walked toward it but as she was almost through, a red-hot lance seared into her brain and she let out a scream of pain.

You're not in control here, a cold voice said inside her head.

"Neither are you," she replied but she was already turning back. Bending to pick up the knife.

"No!" she screamed and put every effort she had into stopping her body.

They came to a stalemate, and she froze in the small dark

garden like some android that was going into meltdown. Part of her knew that this must look a ridiculous sight. A grown woman moving back and forth as she tried to reach down and then held back. She had the sudden urge to laugh, except this situation wasn't funny.

Her arm stretched forward and she bit her cheek. The pain centered her and she stopped. Like a statue, bent over with her right arm stuck out. There she stayed for a few seconds, shaking and rocking on the spot as she forced Matron to relinquish control.

Sweat was running down her forehead and down her back. She felt so dirty, and stale; her clothes were damp and sticky, but she wouldn't give in.

Once more she bit down on her lip. This time on the outside, and she felt her teeth cut through the flesh. It hurt like a mother, but gave her the edge and she straightened up just a little.

Had she won? Maybe if she caused so much pain then Matron would have no control. Maybe that was her way to fight.

No the voice was angry and it sent a shiver down her spine.

You have no chance, for I can wait and I can cause you much more pain than you can cause me.

Once more, white heat seared through her brain. Closing her eyes she reached for her head, but her arms were moving in the opposite direction. While she felt as if she were holding her head, she was vaguely aware of her body reaching down and picking up the knife.

"No!" she screamed, and bit down on her lip once more, but this time her teeth wouldn't move. The pain in her head spread and she screamed silently as her body moved forward.

Shut down and escape the pain, Matron said in a soft, cajoling voice.

It was alluring and Rosie so wanted to comply. To let go of this pain was so enticing. She would do anything to escape the feeling that hot metal had been poured into her skull and was melting her brain… only she couldn't. If she did, then Matron had full use of her body and would do whatever she wanted. If she did, then this woman would die.

Clenching her jaws, she screamed out her agony, and it helped. She knew that she must sound like some wailing banshee and hoped that someone would come. Maybe they could stop her. Maybe she would be arrested and that would be a good thing. If she went to jail then no innocents would have to die.

So she screamed and fought, but it made no difference. Her hand had hold of the knife now.

Slowly, it was raised above the woman's head and then Matron stopped. She reached out and turned the woman, adjusting the direction in which she was standing. Rosie didn't fully understand, but she could tell from the thoughts in her mind that this was important.

Still she fought, and as the hand holding the knife started to lower, she applied everything she had.

In her head something tore and it felt as if blood gushed out and filled her brain. The pressure on her eyes was tremendous and tears were running down her face.

No matter how she tried, she was failing. "Run!" she shouted but she didn't know if the words were only in her mind.

They were answered with a deep and dark chuckle. Matron knew she had won.

Rosie was pushed from control and floating in a sea of pain. Vaguely aware of Matron, she could see and feel a bolt of blue energy entering the index finger of her left hand and heard Matron calling. The language was one she didn't understand. It felt guttural and dirty on her tongue and she had the urge to spit out the words.

Panic seared through her brain along with the pain. The panic that she must do something, stop something, but she couldn't understand why and she was slowly floating away… away from the pain, from the blinding blue light, from the name on her lips —Lucifer.

The knife tore down and she saw the woman's eyes widened as it struck home. Her fist hit flesh and warm blood spread across her hand.

Revulsion brought bile to her throat and yet there was a sense of euphoria, the likes of which she had never experienced. A sense of power so strong, it jerked her upright and threw her back. Held there on a tidal wave of power, she closed her eyes and drank in the life-force. As it began to fade, Rosie pulled back, pulled away from Matron in her mind.

The old lady crumpled to the ground, her pink coat soaked with blood. Her birdlike hands were clasping for her neck. As she fell face down into the mud, her long gray hair fanning around her head, Rosie ran from the vision. Inside her mind she fled back to her vault and blessed darkness.

CHAPTER 7

When did the bed get so hard?

Pain throbbed in Rosie's shoulder as bit by bit she struggled out of sleep. Everything was a blur and her eyes would not open. Reaching up, she could feel something dried on her face and covering her eyes. For a moment she wondered if she had gotten really drunk. A distant memory of dried sick on her face flashed through her mind.

Then panic cut through her stomach like a butcher's knife.

Something was wrong, very wrong, but she couldn't remember what.

Still her eyes wouldn't open, and she knew she wasn't at home. Her hands scrubbed at her face and bits of dried something fell from her skin but eventually she could open her eyes.

It didn't help; it was dark — pitch black in fact.

Where was she?

The sound of traffic had her turning her head to the left and she fought down the impending feeling of panic and dread. Something bad had happened, of that she was sure, but she couldn't remember. There was just this sick empty feeling inside. A feeling that she had done something so wrong and that she would have to pay.

Tears came to her eyes and ran down her face, and as they washed the crust off her cheek, they ran into her mouth. Her tears tasted coppery… and then, she knew… she was caked with blood.

Panic brought her to her feet. Her body ached as if she had fought ten rounds with a world champion. Every muscle screamed in protest as she stood and she wavered on her feet.

Is the blood mine? Am I hurt?

As soon as she had the thought, she knew it was wrong. That it would have been easier if it was hers. That it would have been better—but she still she couldn't remember how she got here, or what she had done. She couldn't even remember where she was.

Slowly she began to walk down the street and as she did, she had flashes of memory. There was an old lady in a pink jacket and faded fawn trousers with a tired, wizened face. Frail bird-like hands fluttered against her chest.

Something about the memory brought a tightness to Rosie's chest.

Was the woman hurt? Could she help her?

Shaking her head she searched her memories as she walked, and then she recognized the street and the ginnel that the woman had walked down.

Nausea dropped her head and emptied her stomach onto the pavement. She remembered Matron, the Old Hag that controlled her. She remembered the feel of the knife in her hand. How the handle was warm and wet and how it throbbed in her fingers. Then she remembered the inner fight with Matron and losing. The look in the poor old woman's eyes as the knife hit flesh.

What have I done?

A sob wracked her body and dropped her to her knees. A fresh steam of vomit flooded her throat, bursting out and hitting the cold pavement splashing back to hit her face.

Rosie wanted to lay there and to forget the world. She would have no more part of this. She would never let this beast use her to kill again.

What if she's still alive?

The question brought her to her feet and she searched the street. No one was around. There was no one to help, no one to hide from, another part of her said, *get home, get cleaned up before the body was discovered*.

"No," Rosie shouted and she started to run to the alley. She turned down and raced through the gloom. Going so fast that it felt as if she was falling through the darkness, as if she was rushing toward her doom. Then she saw the gate —slightly ajar.

It was dark, but her eyes were growing accustomed. She peered into the garden. There, crumpled on the ground like a castaway sack was the old woman. She had fallen face down and her hair spread out around her like a halo. In so many ways she looked peaceful, idyllic, at rest.

A pool of blood was soaking into the grass around her neck.

Rosie let out a gasp and dropped to her knees. They sank into a warm wetness and she knew that more blood would be soaking into her clothes.

With a shaky hand she reached out to find the woman's pulse. Only her neck was cold, sticky, and rubbery. Still she searched but there was nothing there. No sign of life, not even a glimmer.

The tears were falling uncontrollably now and Rosie rocked and sobbed in a world of despair.

You have to go, a voice said in her mind, and she wanted to shout at it. To tell Matron to shut up. That she had done enough already but the voice was her own. It was the rational side of her mind that knew she couldn't stop this, but she had to find a way.

Getting up, she gritted her teeth and knew what she had to do. So she hid her thoughts in her vault and started to walk as fast as she could.

When she got to the opposite end of the alley, she turned away from home. Dropping her head, she put her hands in her pockets. The right one touched the knife. It had sliced through the bottom of the pocket and hung against her leg. The blade nicked her index finger but she ignored the pain. Ignored the feeling of blood as it ran down her finger and pooled in her pocket, before running through the hole and dripping down, down, down.

Just keep walking. That was all she had to do. If she could just keep walking for another fifteen minutes then this would all be over.

What are you doing? Matron asked inside her head, but the voice was weak and somnolent-sounding.

I just feel like a walk, Rosie replied, and then shut her thoughts down. She filled her mind with the old woman's face and the bird-like hands that clawed at her chest. They were so small and insignificant, so ineffectual in a fight. Just like those of a dinosaur she had once seen, and it made her feel so sad.

She wanted to ask why. Why had they done this? Why couldn't Matron just be happy with *her* life? But she already knew. The spirit had been getting weaker since they left RedRise house. There was something wrong with her chest and Rosie thought that it would kill her if it was left. For a moment that was what she wanted. To end this. To end the pain and the fear that she would kill someone again, but she didn't know if she could.

Maybe she could step in front of a truck? If she timed it right then it would be instant death. Maybe that was a better way to end this, since Matron always seemed to control her physically when she tried to end her own life.

Never, the lethargic voice said in her mind, but right now it wasn't very convincing.

Rosie knew she just had to bide her time, for she was close now. Excitement caught her breath in her throat and she fought it down. She must not let on about what she was planning.

Just one more street and then she could walk into the police station. They would take one look at her and know that things were bad.

Her clothes, hands, and no doubt face and hair, were covered in blood. They would arrest her and even if Matron took over—if she couldn't tell them what happened, they would put it together when the body was found.

CHAPTER 8

*A*s she turned onto the street the light outside the police station filled her with hope. It was hard to hide her thoughts. Hard to keep her pace even and to control her breathing, but she must.

Matron was tired, resting. No doubt building up her strength. This might be her only chance to do this and she had to take it. The station was close now and her heart kicked up a beat.

Inside her head Matron stirred.

Rosie quickened her pace and whistled in her mind. It was a Beatles melody, but she couldn't think of the title. Maybe that was a good thing. She searched her memory as she quickened her pace. A car pulled past and around the side of the police station. Rosie kept her eyes low and whistled away.

What was that darn tune called?

The police station was four stories high and looked modern

and efficient. The entrance was just another thirty yards along the building. Like a beacon in the darkness, it called to her. There were double sliding doors and behind them, a reception area. It looked as if no one was there, but then she saw movement.

A uniformed officer walked past and disappeared through a door. The urge to run, to shout, was strong, but she fought it down and kept walking.

Taking a breath she whistled some more, that stupid song with no name. All cheery melody with no substance, it felt just like she did.

Letting out a breath she gasped for another. She could do this and she turned toward the door. The reception was empty but she could see a bell on the counter. Just five more steps and she would be through that door and Amy would be safe. The world would be safe.

A knife sliced through her left temple and embedded in her brain. Or at least that was what it felt like.

Staggering she kept moving forward, just a few more paces and she would be home, free – or at least clear of the fear that she would kill again. The police would know what to do. They would stop her, lock her up.

What are you doing? The voice pushed the knife deeper. *Did you really think you could get away with this, that you could turn me in? You are weak, my servant, and you **will** worship me before the year is out.*

Rosie bent over and clenched her fists so tightly that they ached, but the pain would not ease up. She wanted to scream, could swear that she had, and yet she knew her mouth never moved.

All that existed was the pain; like a sea of molten lava it engulfed her brain in its fiery heat and seared away her intentions, her will, and her consciousness, and then there was nothing.

* * *

The deep searing pain woke Rosie, and she knew instantly that something was wrong. It was almost light and even the gloom hurt her eyes. Screwing them shut, she fought back the tears and dragged in a breath, trying to stop the pain.

It was too much.

Something was crushing her brain.

A gasp escaped her and she forced her eyes open bit by dreadful bit. The hand on her brain tightened until she was sure that her head would simply explode. Instead, the pain eased a little and began to dissipate.

What she was lying on was hard and cold, and a bitter wind whipped around her. She tried to sit up. A wave of nausea rushed over her and dragged her head back to the ground. The ground!

As the vomit spewed from her she realized that she was outside. Lying in a back street.

As her surroundings slowly came into focus she let the tears fall.

What had happened? Where was she?

Confusion was like a heavy blanket, like a dark fog. It clouded her thoughts and each time she tried to peer around it, the fog swirled and coalesced and her memories were buried.

But something was dreadfully wrong. Something awful had happened. Rosie could see that her clothes and hands were covered in something brown and dried. The material was stiff and as she moved bits flaked off.

Was it mud?

Maybe she had fallen and hit her head. It made sense and would explain the pain and the filth. Only it didn't explain how she got here or where she fell, more than that it didn't feel right.

There was a deep hole in her stomach. That feeling of impending doom, or the one you get when you have done something terrible. Something you never intended, something you regret.

What had she done?

The sun was rising and as she looked at her hand, she realized that it wasn't mud… it was blood. Her hands and clothes were soaked in blood. She was covered in it.

Why? How?

Something also told her that she had to move. She must get home and change. She must get out of these clothes before she was caught. Or maybe she should go to the hospital.

Rosie jumped to her feet as another thought hit her. What if this was her blood? Had she been hit by a car, or attacked by a madman?

For a second, adrenaline chased insects up and down her arms, raising the hairs and prickling her skin. The idea was plausible, only the sick feeling in her stomach told her that it wasn't right. Even though her body ached as if she had been hit by a truck and her head was now simply throbbing, she knew that wasn't it. Something had happened, something bad. Why couldn't she remember?

Suddenly she wanted to call Amy and she knew she had to get home. If she was found in this state then she would be taken to a hospital, or arrested. Until she knew what had happened that wasn't a good idea.

The street was dark and dreary. The buildings rundown and uncared for. There were no lights on in any of the windows, but the sun would soon be over the horizon. It was rising behind her and it always rose to the front of her property. Instinct told her to go toward it and so she turned around and headed off down the street.

When she got to the end she knew where she was and so she turned left and quickened her pace. It would take her a good half hour to get home and if she didn't hurry, she would start to meet people.

The more she walked the more panic took over, and soon she was running along the street as if the very devil were on her tail. At last she was on her own road and she raced down it and up to the door. Reaching into her grubby and crusty pockets, she felt a knife in one! From the other she pulled out her keys and fell through the door.

Nausea overtook her. She had to get out of these clothes. Bounding up the stairs, she ripped off her coat and threw it onto the bathroom's beige tiled floor. The room was poorly lit as the sun had only just risen, and yet she could see the blood caked into her fingers and nails. Holding her hands out, they shook as she examined them. Thick red lined her nails and coated her fingers. It ran across her hands and up her arms.

Dropping her hands, she ripped off her fleece and t-shirt.

Even her bra was coated in blood. It must have soaked right through her clothes.

Panic spurred her on and she pulled off her jeans. Flakes of dried blood dropped to litter the tiles as she pulled the stiff denim down her legs.

Naked, except for her necklace, she wanted to curl into the corner of the room and hide but she stepped into the shower.

At first the water was cold and the shock helped to clear her head. There was something controlling her. Though she knew it, it sounded crazy in her mind and she couldn't remember what it was.

Who? The voice in her mind asked. Yes it was a who. Someone had done something bad and it wasn't her.

Finally the water was warm and she reveled in its cleansing power. Filling her hands with shower gel, she lathered all over her body. Then she washed her hair and more red ran from her skin and dirtied the white shower. Letting out a cry of despair, she grabbed the back brush and she began to shrub.

The water ran red as the blood sluiced from her and dribbled down the drain. More and more she scrubbed, her hands, arms, back, legs, everywhere she could, she scrubbed until the water ran clean, and then she scrubbed some more. Soon she was red and sore but she couldn't seem to stop.

Why couldn't she remember?

How had she gotten to that street?

What was wrong with her?

Tears began to fall, and she dropped the brush to the base of the shower and let them come. Hugging herself she rocked beneath the hot water and just let go.

It was only when the water turned cold that she came out of her despair.

Reaching up, she turned it off and stepped from the shower. Grabbing a towel she wiped the tears from her face and went into her bedroom. Sitting down on the bed she pulled the towel tight. It was so cold. Her breath misted before her.

Rosie dried quickly as the water turned to ice on her skin.

Dressing in jeans and another fleece she towel-dried her hair. It was stiff as if it was starting to freeze.

Rosie shook her head and walked to the door. The thermostat was downstairs and she planned to go put on the heating. As she stepped onto the stair, a shadow passed the front door.

Freezing on the spot, she let out a breath. It misted before her.

What was going on? Was someone in the house?

"Hello!" she called, and then wished she hadn't. If someone was here she would be best to hide. But, she had to know.

Slowly she walked down the stairs, and the lower she went the colder it got.

Rosie turned the thermostat but it was over 25 before she heard the boiler burst into life. *Why was it so cold? It made no sense.* The sun shone through the window and the day looked nice. There could be a touch of chill but not this much.

Turning to her right, a shadow crossed the room.

Rosie stepped back as the skin prickled on her arms and her chest tightened.

A smoky mist swirled before her forming into the shape of a person. Within the smoke a face appeared. The mouth torn open in a scream. Its eyes were wild. But just as soon as it happened, it was gone and so was the mist.

CHAPTER 9

Rosie sank down into an easy chair, a cheese toasty and a cup of tea precariously perched in her hands.

Her heart was still beating too quickly and there was a sense of something wrong that she couldn't quite put her finger on. Of course, she had come home covered in blood with no memory of how it got there. That was enough to start with. Now she was seeing things... misty shadows with faces in them.

What she wanted to do was ring Amy, to ring her friend, the one who always seemed to know what to do. The one who could cope with anything. But she couldn't even bring herself to do that.

There was a deep fear inside of her. What had happened last night? What had she done? What was she seeing? What were the shadows, were they really there? Maybe she was going mad. Something told her that to call Amy would be wrong. It didn't make sense.

The cheese toasty was cold, stiff and congealed—she couldn't face it. So she picked up the tea, and clinging to the cup like a security blanket, she took a long sip. It was hot, strong, black, and it warmed her as it slipped down her throat.

She needed to get some perspective. Maybe if she relaxed, and let go, then her memories would come back. With that thought in mind, she flicked on the television.

It was on the news channel. An overly cheerful man was making a meal of the weather. Cold, cloudy, some sunny spells, and the chance of some rain. It almost made her laugh as he seemed to have covered every variable.

Next came the headlines. Normally she liked the news, but today she just couldn't concentrate. It all blurred in her mind and she looked down to see her hands shaking and covered in blood.

"No!" She stood up, the tea spilling. Putting the cup down, she held her hands out before her. They were clean. There was no sign of any blood.

A breath came out of her in a long sob. What was happening to her?

Back in the chair she picked up the tea and took another sip. Closing her eyes, she savored the tea. It would calm her, it always did, and yet today not even that seemed to help.

A flash of red spliced through her mind. A face contorted in terror and so much blood. Rosie gasped. The images had come so quickly, and were gone just as soon. They made no sense and yet they scared her. Was this a memory? What had she done?

As if in answer, the local news broadcaster's voice boomed out of the television. He caught her attention and she turned to look at him. He seemed to be staring right at her as he read the news. Was there accusation in his eyes?

"A brutal murder, of a sweet and well-loved local resident took place sometime last night."

The sickness inside Rosie grew until it was everything. *What had she done?*

The report continued, the crime had taken place not a mile from her home and the police were asking for witnesses.

Rosie heard it all and yet she was not there, not present. It was as if she were peering out of a window, looking on at the scene of an accident. None of it made sense and she wanted to scream out her frustration and fear. *What was happening?*

The picture changed as the camera went live to the location. Shocked neighbors were interviewed and all the time Rosie felt the sickness inside.

She recognized this place. She had been there. Again blood filled her vision and she bit her lip to make it go away.

They were showing a picture of an old lady, Mary Price. She had long gray hair and was wearing a threadbare pink coat.

She had seen that coat before, but where?

A smile graced the woman's wrinkled face and all the neighbors told of what a nice lady she had been... always friendly, always helping.

"This is just such a terrible shame," a woman said as she hugged her child to her knees. "Who would do such a thing?"

Deep inside her head Rosie could hear laughter. She shook her head to try and drive the sound away, but it just got louder.

THE BATTLE WITHIN

The television crackled, the lights flickered, and in the corner of the room a shadow appeared.

Rosie shrank back into her chair and clutched onto her head. It hurt, ached, and that laugh just wouldn't stop.

The voice sounded old; maybe it was the voice of the woman, of Mary. Had she killed her? Was she being haunted?

It made no sense. Why would she hurt anyone? Yet deep down inside she had this cold, oily, dread. She knew that she had done something terrible.

You did kill her.

The voice was inside her own head, and yet it was not her voice.

A shadow appeared in the corner.

"Stop it," Rosie shouted, but she didn't know who she was shouting at. Was this her own voice, her own madness? It made no sense.

The light continued to flicker and the room chilled. Her breath steamed before her and in the corner of the room the shadow deepened, thickened. What was once translucent gained shape and form. A smoky figure appeared: a frail, small, human. Then it was gone.

Remember.

The word was said inside her head, by that same old and dreadful voice. Everything came back to her. It was like a whirlwind of sounds, shapes, smells, sensations, and emotions. She dropped to her knees, and before she could stop it, vomited the tea onto the floorboards.

"You did this," she said the words aloud. "You killed her. You killed Mary. Why?"

Because I needed power. Now I have it, and soon I will have more, Matron answered back.

It was such a strange sensation. Her own mouth opening and closing and speaking a voice that was not her own.

"No, oh my God no! You killed her, you killed her. How could you, how could you do this. You killed the woman in the pink coat. I won't let you do this again, never again."

I will do it again. I will kill anyone I want and I will do it whenever I want.

"No, no, not with me. I will stop you. Even if it kills me, I will stop you."

No you won't. You will worship me and I will kill your friends, every single one of them, including Amy.

Rosie let out a scream of anger and despair. Now she remembered everything. How she was conned in RedRise House. How she was taken over by the spirit of Old Hag, who now called herself Matron. She even remembered last night. The excitement as they stalked Mary down the street. The fear in the old woman's eyes. How her bird-like hands had clawed at her throat and how wonderful it all felt.

It hadn't been her excitement, her wonder, no, it was Matron's, but feeling it now turned her stomach.

Would she be able to stay in control? Would she be able to prevent this creature from killing again? Would she be able to save Amy?

A knock on the door sent a jolt of fear down her spine.

"No!" she screamed, for she knew it was Amy coming to check on her. How could she drive her friend away?

* * *

AMY SKIPPED down the street looking forward to seeing her friend. Only she was worried about Rosie. Something had been dreadfully off the night before. It was almost as if her friend wasn't herself.

Of course, she had to realize that Rosie had been through a lot. Maybe sending her to that remote house had been a mistake. Well, she was back now. Clive was locked up, and Rosie could start to rebuild her life.

Amy walked up to the white door and was about to knock. The sound of shouting froze her in place.

Rosie never shouted. She also had no other friends. Clive had managed to isolate her from everyone. Had driven them all away, all except her. It made no sense that Rosie would be talking to someone, shouting at someone.

Worried, she was about to burst in, but something stopped her. Was it fear?

It sounded as if Rosie was shouting at herself. The second voice was different but it was still Rosie's. She was shouting something about killing and stopping. Amy pressed her ear to the door.

"I will kill your friends, every single one of them including Amy."

Amy stepped back. Had she really heard that? It had to have been a mistake. For a moment she stood there, her hand poised on the handle. Muttering came from within but she couldn't make it out. Part of her wanted to leave but she would never do that, so she knocked, and taking a deep breath, walked in.

The door opened into a small entrance hall, with just enough room to close the door. The stairs were in front of her, to the left the kitchen, to the right the living room. The shouting had been coming from her right but Amy couldn't move.

Right in front of her eyes, on the pale cream wall leading up the stairs was a bloody handprint.

CHAPTER 10

Rosie heard the door open. What could she do? Inside her head Matron was shouting.

Kill her, kill her, kill her now!

"No I won't."

Pain filled her mind. Like molten lava, it seared through her brain and it was everything. Amy was forgotten. Matron was forgotten. Her whole world was pain and fire.

Against her will, her body moved. The motions jerky and robotic as Matron tried to regain control.

Rosie knew she had to do something. She knew it was something important, but she couldn't get past the pain. In her own living hell, she floated on a sea of agony. It consumed her mind, her body, her everything.

Matron smiled. She was gaining control. Unfortunately, Rosie was stronger than she had expected, and the woman was fiercely protective of her friend. It didn't matter. Matron's strength would grow with each kill, and soon she would be in total control. Getting rid of Amy was only the beginning. Without that tie to her humanity, Rosie would fail.

Matron lurched toward the knife. She had heard Amy come in but had heard nothing since. Where had the infuriating woman gone?

The knife was on a coffee table. Just five steps away. With the pain she was inflicting on Rosie it should have been easy, and yet her host fought it. Every step was difficult and she needed to hurry. The fight continued, but she was winning. The pain was wearing Rosie down, and with every step, Rosie's resolve failed. It would take just one more and she could reach down for the knife.

Her hand moved out and she bent to clasp it.

"No," Rosie screamed.

The voice was strong in her head. Much too strong. Sending another wave of pain weakened her, but it drove the voice away. Confident now, she reached down to grab the knife.

The touch of the knife gave her strength. The familiar feel of the damp leather. The weight of the blade and the way it glinted. Catching the nearest bit of light and reflecting it, magnifying it, not with brightness but with darkness and despair. Euphoria went through her as she imagined slashing Amy's throat. She could feel the splash of warm blood, could taste the salty goodness and feel the strength it gave her.

Where was her visitor?

So far Amy had come into the house, but where was she?

Matron walked toward the entrance. Her footsteps loud on the old floorboards. If Amy was there she knew she was coming. A snarl started in her throat but she bit it down. Amy was not expecting trouble, she had come to see her friend. Forcing a smile on her face, she walked forward more confidently. It was difficult, Rosie was still fighting, but she was getting weaker. The voice inside her head fading while the screams grew louder. That brought a genuine smile to her face. Rosie was inside her own hell. Forced to burn for as long as Matron kept the pressure on. It took a lot out of her. Sweat was running down her back, and down her forehead, but for now it was worth it.

"Amy is that you?" Matron called in a voice as light as she could manage.

There was no answer. Did the woman know? Was she waiting? Was she ready for her?

It didn't matter. Matron needed more souls. Fighting Rosie was harder than she could ever imagine, and she knew that Amy was the key to her success. Her death would be the end of her friend.

That thought brought a feeling of warmth to her and the smile on her face was once more genuine.

Matron rounded the corner to see Amy staring at the wall. The shock on her face was pure and laughable. Matron's eyes followed Amy's. There on the insipid cream wall was a bloody handprint.

Matron clenched her jaw. It was a foolish mistake. Why had she left it? Damn Rosie, she was hiding things from her. This had to stop.

The knife was held behind her back. Weighing it in her hand she approached. This was the part she loved. Stalking the victim. Knowing that she would take their life in an instant.

Keeping a smile on her face, she watched her prey for any sign of panic.

Amy just looked shocked, as if she didn't know what to do.

This would be easier than Matron had hoped.

It would take just two more steps. She hefted the knife in her hand. Getting ready to move forward. One step with her left foot and then she would swing the knife as her right foot traveled forward. The arc was perfect. The knife would slash right to left, severing the jugular and spraying her with blood. It would be messy, but that didn't matter. Rosie lived like a recluse. No one was going to see it.

Amy turned. Her eyes narrowed and her mouth opened, but nothing came out.

Matron congratulated herself. This was perfect. Should she allow Rosie to see? Should she reduce the pain?

For a moment she wavered on the spot, hesitating, trying to decide if she should inflict this greater torture. No. Rosie would see it through her eyes for years to come so there was no point in taking the risk now.

She smiled a crocodile smile and stepped forward with her left foot.

Amy returned the smile and looked a little better. A little more relaxed. Matron began the final assault and could feel her victory. She stepped forward with her right foot and began to swing out her arm with the knife.

Pain seared through her mind and she lost control. At the last moment, she flung herself at Amy and pulled the girl into her arms. Matron screamed as Rosie took control. She screamed against the pain and the impotence of the moment, but it didn't help. Rosie was back in control.

"It's so good to see you," Rosie said, and hugged her friend tightly, the knife clasped behind Amy's back.

Matron could feel her joy and it sickened her, but she knew that this wouldn't last. She would regain control and next time Amy would die.

* * *

Rosie fought the pain, controlled it, mastered it, and sent it back at Matron just at the last moment. Surging forward she widened the arc on her arm and pulled Amy into her arms. Hiding the knife behind her friends back. How could she get Amy out of here? How could she explain and get her help? Whatever she did, her friend would be in danger and would no doubt think her mad.

It didn't matter for now. Amy was safe, and maybe she could get her help; she just had to work out how.

"Are you going to tell me about this and the mumbling?" Amy said pointing at the bloody hand print.

"Mumbling?" Rosie said the word before she could stop it. Matron was testing her. She bit her lip and forced her back.

"Rosie, Your lip!"

"I'm just so nervous, so wired." Looking at the hand print and she almost cried. If she told Amy the truth then Matron would come back, would kill her friend. How she knew that she couldn't say but she did. "I fell, cut myself," was all she could manage as she led her friend to the kitchen.

Soon they were seated in the small kitchen drinking tea.

Rosie clung to her cup as if it were a lifeline and she was drowning. She could see Amy was worried, but her friend waited, expecting her to talk. What could she say?

Rosie bit her lip once more and let out a breath.

"Your lip!" Amy said.

Rosie reached up and touched her lip. It was damp she stared at her fingers. They were covered in blood. Both hands covered in blood, so much of it. Running over her fingers and dripping onto the worn oak table.

Rosie jerked to a stand and the flimsy chair fell back and rattled as it hit the cream tiled floor. There was blood everywhere. Of course there was… she had killed a woman.

"Rosie!"

Amy's voice pierced through her panic and Rosie looked at her hands. There was a small droplet of blood on her fingers from her lip. The constant biting of her lip was making it sore and that was all she had seen, wasn't it?

Tears came to her eyes and she lowered her head to hide them. Picking up the chair, she slumped back into it and laid her head on her arms. "You should go," she mumbled. "I'm not feeling well."

A hand touched her arm and Rosie jumped.

You need to kill her, she suspects, a faint voice said in her head.

Rosie looked up and Amy was leaning over her. She looked so concerned; her big, brown eyes were drawn down and her pink lips clenched with worry. "Tell me what's wrong. Who were you talking to?"

"Nothing… it's… something happened at RedRise House."

Pain lanced through her brain and she let out a cry of anguish.

"Rosie what is it?" Amy asked, still holding her arm.

"Headaches. I just keep getting headaches now. Why won't you go and leave me alone."

"Because I care for you and you're not telling me everything."

You need to kill her, do it now, Matron's voice was stronger, more insistent, and Rosie shook her head to drive it away.

She had pushed the knife down the back of her jeans and she could feel the cold of the blade against her back. She wanted to reach around and grab it. To plunge it into Amy – No, no, no what was wrong her?

"You have to go," Rosie said and she looked up at her friend, her eyes pleading with all she had.

Amy just smiled.

"I'm not leaving you when you need me."

Kill her, if she finds out you will go to jail, do you want that? Matron asked and pushed against Rosie's mind.

Rosie felt her right hand move. It twitched and slid off the table. She tried to stop it but it wouldn't obey. Sitting up, she pushed Amy's arm away.

"You have to leave!" Rosie shouted, and she watched Amy shy back. "I am dangerous. Something happened at that house, something bad and I..." Rosie intended to say I killed someone, but the words had frozen in her throat. She was losing control. Matron was coming back. "I want to hurt myself when I'm alone." No, this was the last thing she wanted to say. It would make Amy stay, and the longer she stayed the more danger she was in.

"Rosie stop talking like this," Amy said, coming around the table, she crouched next to her and pulled her into her arms. "I know you have been through so much, but I am here for you for as long as you want. Tell me what's bothering you."

Matron smiled inside of Rosie and she knew that she would soon lose control. Would she kill her friend and wake up covered in her blood? She had to do something. Maybe she could take her own life. It would be awful and Amy would never forgive herself but at least she would be alive.

Matron was fighting in Rosie's mind, trying to work out what to say and trying to gain control. The knife stuck to her back and she knew it had nicked the skin. She could feel a trickle of blood as it ran down between her buttocks. It was warm and she so wanted to feel it in her hand. She licked her lip in anticipation, but caught herself and turning the lick into a bite, she chomped down on her lip. The pain brought her back a touch of control but blood ran from her lip.

"Stop it," Amy said. "Stop this and talk to me."

Matron laughed inside and Rosie felt her control slipping just a little bit more. "Run," she shouted, "Amy please run." Only the words never passed her lips, for Matron was getting stronger.

CHAPTER 11

Rosie felt the blood run from her lip and she could see the concern in Amy's eyes. Her friend had stepped away from her and for the first time since they had met, she looked unsure.

Rosie fought for control and she knew she was shaking. She must look strange as she shook her head to get rid of the influence of the spirit. "I won't give in," she said. "You can't have her I will never kill for you again."

"Yes you will. I am in control and you will worship me," Matron replied her voice deeper more, guttural in Rosie's mouth.

"Rosie what are you saying?" Amy asked. "Stop this and talk to me."

Rosie looked at her friend. "You have to leave for your own safety. You have to go."

"Don't be silly. You need my help." Amy took a step closer to Rosie.

This is not me, Rosie shouted, but the words were never spoken aloud; they stayed inside her mind as Matron took control. Rosie waved her arms wide and shook her head.

Amy's eyes were wide as she stared in horror.

How she wanted to tell her friend everything. To tell her that she had killed. To tell her to call the police that they would find the knife in the back of her jeans and her bloody clothing upstairs—but she couldn't. Instead, she sat in the chair and shook. Her eyes rolled back into her head and her body convulsed as Matron fought for control.

Rosie knew she was losing, that Amy would be killed, and a tear escaped her eyes and ran down her cheek. What could she do?

The temperature dropped in the room and Amy's breath steamed before her. Rosie watched as her friend rubbed her arms. Her mouth opening and closing, Amy took out her phone. For a moment she stared at it. "Let me take you to to the Doc's," she said and held the phone out as if it would somehow help.

Behind Amy, Rosie saw a shadow, a darkness, and she understood. Inside the shadow was the faint tinge of pink. The faint outline of a faded pink jacket. The padded kind that keeps you warm. The type a poor old lady would wear. The type Mary had worn last night.

As the spirit manifested, Matron lost a little of her grip. Rosie let out a breath that misted before her and she pointed.

Amy turned around.

In the corner of the kitchen there was a darkness, a smoky outline that coalesced and wavered, and then a faint figure emerged from the shadow.

Amy let out a breath and stared, her jaw dropping almost to the floor.

Rosie knew it was the old woman, Mary. Had she come to help her? Her arrival seemed to create a static charge in the air and Matron had shrank away. That made no sense. Matron had bragged that the souls she took gave her strength.

The shadow moved like insects swarming, changing shape and size. Now it was just a moving black cloud… and then a face appeared. It was contorted into a scream, and Rosie felt her stomach flip as she knew that was the moment the knife had hit home.

It felt like she was there forever, but the apparition was gone within milliseconds and the room returned to normal.

"You have to go," Rosie said, and Amy turned around to look at her. There was confusion and fear in her eyes. Rosie was pleased with that. If she could frighten Amy away, that was a good thing.

"What... what was that?"

Rosie felt another tear leave her eye. She knew she had to help Mary, had to send her back like she had the children, and to do that, she had to stay out of prison. Maybe prison wouldn't hold Matron anyway. She had to stay strong and destroy this bitch who had ruined her life, and to do that she had to get help.

"It was a ghost; it came back with me from RedRise House."

Amy sat back down in her chair. Her mouth opening and closing but she said nothing.

"Amy, I need help," Rosie said, "and I need you to believe me."

"Rosie, you're making no sense. A ghost, these crazy words, is this about Clive? If it is, you are safe. He's in jail and he will never hurt you again."

Rosie wanted to scream. To shout, *listen to me,* but she could feel her control slipping and she could feel her right arm inching around to the knife. Clenching her jaw tightly, she fought it and the urge to stab was gone. But, Matron was still here, and the battle inside was in full flow. It was like a banshee inside her head. Wailing and clawing and shouting at her. The noise, the pain, the clamor was too much and suddenly, all she wanted to do was sleep.

"I need your help," she managed and then her control slipped. "I need you to understand I'm just tired and distressed. Maybe if you stay with me for a while I will feel better," Matron said, and gave Amy a sickly smile.

"Of course," Amy said. "You go into the living room and put on a DVD. I will make us a couple of mochas and we can order a curry. What do you say?"

Rosie shook her head and shouted *go, go, just get out of here,* but the words never left her mind. She felt her lips pull back into a smile that felt more like a snarl. "That sounds great," Matron said.

Rosie collapsed onto the worn pink sofa and fought a silent battle. Matron was pushing, fighting, and clawing for control, but she managed to retain at least partial use of her limbs. Leaning back she relaxed as much as she could, pretending that she was tiring, for she had a plan.

Amy came through a few minutes later and put two cups on the coffee table. "What are we watching?" she asked.

"Watching?" Matron's guttural voice asked. Rosie kept quiet, let her show her ignorance.

"What film do you fancy?"

"Film?"

"If you're too tired we can just sit and read or talk."

"No," Rosie managed, and whispered in Matron's head. "We should watch a moving picture. I've seen one of them before." Matron smiled at Rosie's cooperation and grinned at Amy as she repeated the words.

"Which one?" Amy asked her eyebrows drawn down in confusion at the term.

Doubt filled Matron's mind, she really didn't understand but Rosie had drawn back into her vault. She would watch and monitor. She would ensure that Amy stayed safe, but she wouldn't assist. For a moment, there was pain and Rosie let out a yelp.

"Rosie what is it?" Amy asked.

"Nothing, just flashbacks."

"I understand, why don't I choose the film?"

Matron nodded, and Rosie was engulfed in the sense of smug satisfaction.

Amy put on the latest Star Wars DVD. It was one that Rosie had been looking forward to watching, but she could hardly hear a word. The constant battle for control was exhausting. But if she let up on her guard, then she knew that Matron would kill Amy, and she couldn't allow that.

After twenty minutes the curries arrived. They went to the kitchen and Rosie stood back while Amy got plates from the cupboard. Once more she could feel her hand itching to go around for the knife.

It took every ounce of control to stop it, and she knew that she was shaking again.

Amy pulled her into her arms and hugged her tightly. "Oh Rosie, I'm so sorry that this is so bad for you. I'd really hoped that you would be better away from everything. Now I think it has caused you so much stress. I will never forgive myself for making things worse."

Rosie wanted to hug her back but she remained stiff in Amy's arms. The urge to stab Amy was overwhelming, and she had to bite down on her lip to stop her right hand from reaching out for the knife. Little by little she regained some control and when she did, she pulled away.

"Just give me a moment," she said, and ran from the room. Once up the stairs, she pulled the knife from her trousers and threw it onto the bloody clothes which lay crumpled in the corner. Tears ran down her face. What could she do?

Should she just sit in the corner and hope Amy would leave?

No, that was no good. She had to get her friend to go, and if she stayed here, then Amy would come up to help. Then she remembered her plan. It was weak but it was all she had.

Wiping her face, she went down the stairs and together they would eat the curry.

Rosie let her exhaustion pull her back to her vault. She let Matron take over, for she was sure that the curry would not be something she would want.

CHAPTER 12

"What is that awful smell?" Matron asked as she came into the kitchen.

"It's your favorite," Amy said. "Jalfrezi and a garlic naan.

Amy was busy serving up the dishes and arranging them on trays. She tried to be upbeat and friendly, but the strain was showing and exhaustion hung heavily on her. Finally grabbing a couple of beers from the fridge, she opened the bottles and placed one on each tray.

Rosie was staring at the tray, her lips curled back in either disgust or a snarl. It was hard to tell.

"What's wrong?" Amy asked, as she picked up her own tray.

"Wrong? Why do you keep asking what's wrong?"

"Because you are acting so strangely. Rosie, talk to me. Why don't we forget the film and sit here and talk? Maybe I can help you."

Amy watched her friend waver on the spot. Quickly, she put

her own tray on the table and grabbed Rosie's arm. It was cold and stiff. "Come on, take a seat." She guided Rosie to the small table and sat her down.

Bringing both of the meals over, she took a seat opposite Rosie. "You need to eat; you look as if you're losing weight and frankly you look haggard."

Rosie had been staring at the curry as if it was something a dog had left on the pavement. She lifted her head and the malice in her eyes almost pushed Amy from her chair. There was something cold, something cruel in that look, and it was the exact opposite of what she expected from her friend. For a moment, Amy thought about leaving and never coming back. She shook her head and let out a sigh.

"Damn it Rosie, talk to me!"

"What do you wish me to say?" Rosie asked.

"Tell me what is wrong?"

"I just wish to be treated with more respect... with the respect I deserve."

Amy shook her head again. It was a strange thing for her friend to say. "I'm sorry, I do respect you and I worry... I heard you talking earlier... about killing, and I'm really worried about you."

For long moments Rosie just stared and Amy felt her stomach tighten. It was as if her friend was staring her down, like she was challenging her and expecting her to back down. Then Rosie relaxed.

"I'm a writer, remember. I was just doing a bit of character work. Plotting out aloud."

Amy smiled, that made sense, but it didn't ring true. Rosie

wrote sweet historical romances and she was quite sure there had never been a murder in any of her books. "Okay, but if anything else is bothering you, I can help."

"I know, and I will inform you when I need your assistance."

Once more the tone was so cold, formal, calculating, and downright insulting. What was wrong with Rosie?

Amy picked at her food and watched as Rosie did the same. Each time Rosie took a mouthful she grimaced. They had eaten this meal on many occasions and Rosie had always loved it.

Amy opened her mouth to ask what was wrong, but for some reason she decided it was best to let it be. Maybe Rosie was just tired, maybe it was something more, but pushing her wasn't going to help.

So they ate in silence, and the longer it went on the more uncomfortable the silence became. In the end, Amy knew she was best to leave and come back in a day or two. Maybe her friend would be more herself then. Yet she also had a strange feeling that she shouldn't leave. That Rosie really needed her —but it didn't make a lot of sense.

"Is there anything else I can do for you?" Amy asked, as she tidied away the plates.

Rosie sat at the table and started to shake. Her hand went around behind her and she snapped it back. Staring at it, as she held it out in front of her. All the color had run from her cheeks and she looked deathly ill.

"Rosie?"

Amy ran to her side and touched her.

Rosie struck out and pushed her away.

"Rosie, damn it, talk to me!"

Rosie looked up, her face contorted and morphed. It was as if two people inside of her were battling. One wanted to smile the other was angry. They fought for control of her face and her whole body went stiff. She clenched her fists and teeth.

"Rosie what is it?" Amy backed away a little and the room turned cold once more. Behind Rosie, a shadow formed in the doorway. A misty shape loomed toward them and then was gone so quickly she wondered if it had been real.

Amy wanted to run, wanted to rush forward and hold Rosie; instead she stood rock still on the spot. Something strange was going on here, but what?

Rosie got up. "You should be going now, but before you do I have something for you to do." Rosie walked across the room and picked up a pen. Then she searched through the kitchen drawer until she found out some postcards. Pulling one out, she wrote on it and handed it over with a wink.

Amy took the card and held it in her hand. The moment was surreal. Rosie was trying to tell her something but she didn't know what. At last she glanced at the card. It read,

Computer for sale £3000. Call Rosie.

Amy opened her mouth to say something, but Rosie gave her their secret wink once more. The one that said I know I'm telling a little white one, but work with me. They had used this code so many times, but never like this. It was always to hide something from someone else. Never anything bad. It was usually when Rosie was mentoring a youngster and she didn't want to hurt their feelings.

Again Amy tried to formulate a question. This was obviously

not a real advert. There were no details, no phone number, £3000, so what was the purpose of it?

"Can you put it in the window of the high-street post office? You know the one you pass on your way home, she asked Amy?"

Even that didn't make sense. Amy's way home was in the opposite direction, but suddenly she felt excitement surge through her. Rosie wanted her to see something in that post office window and this was the only way she could tell her. Amy nodded. "Sure. Do you want me to come see you tomorrow?"

"Ye... no..." Rosie's face contorted again. It was as if she was trying to stop the words. For a moment she looked old and Amy gasped, but the visage was gone as quickly as it appeared and once again it was just her friend, looking pale and exhausted. "No, why don't you come back when you have some news from the card?"

"Of course," Amy said, and she headed to the door. In the hallway, she looked at the bloodstained handprint on the wall and she knew she had to go. "See you soon," she called, and rushed through the door.

Once outside, she let out a big breath. It was dark now and cold, but not as cold as it had been in the kitchen earlier. What in the world had just happened?

For a moment she hesitated on the spot. Should she call the doctor, and ask him to come out and see Rosie? Should she go back in? Something was dreadfully wrong and yet – the card weighed heavily in her hand. Rosie had tried to tell her something.

Climbing into her car, she drove in the opposite direction to home, straight to the post office.

When she got there she pulled up outside and sat in the car. The post office was already closed for the night but she had to assume that Rosie wanted her to see one of the advertisements in the window. Now all she had to do was work out which one. For a moment she closed her eyes and tried to go back through the whole visit. It was surreal, creepy even.

Had the temperature really dipped? Had she seen a shadow in the corner? What was it? Why was Rosie acting so weird?

Nothing made sense, and the more she thought, the more her head hurt. In exasperation, she got out of the car and went to the window. There, on the left-hand side, was a panel with cards like the one Rosie had given her. Each one was an advertisement for second-hand goods or for services.

There was a cleaner advertising her services and Amy wished she had the money to hire her. A smile crossed her face as she imagined coming home to a clean and sweet smelling house. She let out a breath and looked at the other cards. There was a sofa for sale, a chair and some tables, two cars, two bikes, and a handyman offering his services. Then at the bottom she saw it, and her heart nearly stopped. Could this be what Rosie wanted her to see? She thought about the shape, the darkness that formed and looked like a... like a shadow... like a ghost.

The advert read:

The Spirit Guide
Are you dealing with unexplained encounters?
Cold spots, whispers, feelings of dread.
With a PhD in paranormal studies, we can help you.

When no one else believes you, we will.
Call Jesse and Gail
On 07739 xxx xxx
Or email Jesse@thespiritguide.co.uk

FOR A MOMENT she shook her head and went back to the other adverts. One by one she went over them all, but this was the only one that could be relevant. Suddenly she was laughing. The more she laughed the more ridiculous it seemed. This advert relevant, how could those two thoughts be in the same sentence? She laughed some more and bent over holding her side.

Rosie couldn't really expect her to call this pair of charlatans, could she?

In her mind she saw the handprint and the shadow in the corner. She felt the chill on her skin and saw how her breath had misted before her. What was going on?

Quickly she took a photo of the advert with her phone and then she was back in the car and driving home. It seemed so surreal, and the further she drove from the post office the more she thought it must have been a joke. That had to be it. Rosie was playing a prank on her. The incident at her house must have been staged – and yet, Rosie was not like that. What was going on?

CHAPTER 13

All around her was darkness. Fear rushed in from all sides. It surrounded her. Pressed down on her. Crushed her chest and forced the air from her lungs. Panic, like a wild bird *flapping* against a window – trapped, terrified – it consumed her.

Where was she? How had she got here?

The thoughts were fleeting and she tried to shrink down inside herself. To be so small that she would not be seen, not be found. Inside she could hear Matron, stirring, waking. Had the woman brought her here? She must have, and yet Rosie was back in control, even if only for a little while.

The beating of her heart was like a fist against her chest. Blood rushed through her ears and for a moment, the world swam before her. Closing her eyes, she fought for control and steadied herself.

Gradually she was becoming accustomed to the darkness and she recognized where she was.

This was the passage beneath RedRise House. Behind her she could hear running water from the underground stream. To her right would be the alcove where she had found the book. The one that told her all about Matron, the Old Hag who now possessed her. Which meant, in front of her was a door.

As her eyes adjusted, she could make out the door. From beneath it, light flickered and taunted her. Fear reared inside her like a terrified horse; she reined it in and rode it down. If she let her fear win then she would die here, or worse than that she would kill.

The sound of chanting came from behind the door. For a moment she looked behind her. Should she run or should she go forward? It was an impossible choice and yet she felt pulled toward that door.

Before she knew that she was moving forward, her hand touched the cold handle. It opened easily, much smoother than she expected. Dipping her head, she walked through. The sacrificial chamber was just as she remembered. Dark and dismal, but lighted by four flaming torches.

Across the room, two tall figures were cloaked in black. All around them over a dozen children of all ages stood facing away from her. Torchlight danced across the walls, making shadows of the figures trace over the cold and dismal stone.

They were chanting. It was in Latin and she could not pick out the words, but the meaning of the chant was clear. It was an offering. Rosie knew that behind the figures was a sacrificial stone. On top of it, somebody would be tied. Their life would soon be over, their last moments, filled with terror.

"No!" the word was out before she could stop it.

Silence descended on the cellar.

Monstrous shadows loomed at her as the figures turned. Their gaze pinpointed her in the darkness like a spotlight on Karaoke night.

Why was she here? What was she doing?

Rosie wanted to run, to flee from that place and to never come back, but she knew that was not an option. The last time she was here she couldn't leave. The house wouldn't let her leave. Why would it be different this time?

The children surged forward and crowded around her. It was hard to see them in the flickering light but her mind filled in the blanks. She had met them before. Their bodies would be thin and dirty. Their eyes, sunken into their heads, would reflect the torture they had suffered. But that was not what she feared to see.

Pulling her eyes from the children, she looked at the two hooded figures. They stood back waiting, their heads bowed as if in respect. They thought she was Matron.

Maybe she could use that to her advantage. Maybe she could save whoever was on the altar.

As she had the thought, a high pitched keening sound started in the cellar.

Rosie knew it was the children, but she refused to look down.

The noise grew louder, higher, so piercing that it hurt her ears.

With her heart pounding so hard she thought it would burst from her chest, her eyes were pulled down to the children. Though she didn't want to look, she had no choice.

THE BATTLE WITHIN

One by one each of them looked up at her. Their heads back exposing their throats.

Rosie let out a scream. Each of their throats had been slit. The noise was not coming from their mouths. It was coming from the gaping wound in their necks that opened and closed in time to the terrible noise.

"No," Rosie let out the word and dropped to the floor. It was cold, wet, and slimy. It felt like skin covered with blood – she jumped back to her feet.

Now the two cloaked figures stared at her strangely. They moved toward her along with the children.

Hands reached out to touch her. They grabbed her clothes, reached for her hands, and clawed at her body. Some were so small that she wanted to hold them. To pull the children into her arms and to tell them all would be well, but she couldn't. All was not well. She had to save whoever was on the altar. Then she would send as many of these children to peace as she could before Matron regained control.

She shook her head as if clearing her thoughts. Putting a neutral expression on her face, she stood and walked toward the altar.

The way cleared before her. The children and the two acolytes drew back, with reverence, to let her pass.

Rosie's chest tightened with fear. It was hard to breathe, hard to walk, hard to keep up the ruse – but she had to. There, tied on the altar was a young girl. She looked about eight. Her body so thin, her clothes merely rags.

Behind Rosie, the two acolytes began to chant once more and the terrible keening noise dropped down to a mere whisper.

Rosie could see the fear in the girl's eyes. They were as wide as saucers and they pleaded with her for mercy. She wanted to let the child know she would save her but she couldn't… not just yet.

Somehow she had to get the girl out of here and then a plan formed in her mind.

Turning suddenly, she let fury cross her face.

"How dare you bring me one who is impure!" she shouted at the acolytes.

The chanting stopped and they backed away from her. It was working.

"I will not have her defiling this sacred place. Will not have her blood spilled. Get her away from here… now!"

The two cloaked figures looked at each other and then back at Rosie. She kept her face screwed into a snarl. Kept the anger clear in her eyes. *It was going to work.*

The two acolytes cleared a path through the children and to the altar.

Rosie felt a sense of joy knowing that she had done something good. She searched her mind for the releasing ritual she had used before. The one she had used to send the children to peace. The one she would use now for as long as she could.

But, something was awakening inside of her. Like a slippery snake it curled inside her mind. Growing, pushing, and forcing part of her away.

A laugh echoed within her and she knew that Matron was back.

Not now, she said inside her mind. *Not now; I won't allow you to come back now.*

You have no choice. I am stronger than you and growing even stronger by the minute.

Pain ripped through her mind causing her to scream and drop to her knees. Clenching her teeth she pushed the pain away and fought against Matron. It was like a pushing match, like arm wrestling between minds. Rosie pushed, Matron pushed back. Rosie ground her heels into the ground and pushed. She gritted her teeth and gave it all she had.

It was no use. A ripping, tearing seemed to split her head in half and Matron surged through. Rosie was floating in a sea of pain. Watching as Matron grinned and took control.

"Stop!" the guttural voice came out of Rosie's mouth. "The girl is pure and her soul is mine."

Rosie felt the warm slick leather of the knife in her hand. Watched as it was raised above her.

The acolytes were chanting now. Rosie thrashed against her mind, fighting to regain control of her arm, but to no avail. She was screaming, "No, no, no, no!"

Over and over again she screamed as the knife plunged down into the young girl. Her hand hit flesh and was covered in blood as the knife went clean through the girl's throat. Creating an extra mouth just like all the other kids had.

Rosie screamed and fought, she was lying on her back. Back in control again, she searched the darkness in confusion. Was it too late for the girl?

As her eyes adjusted, she let out a long breath. She was lying on her bed, drenched in sweat. Had it all been a dream… just a nightmare, or was it a memory?

As the dream left her, faded, she lay on the bed, panting. Little by little her heart returned to a normal beat and she could breathe more easily.

Had Matron done this to her? Was it another form of torture, or had it just been a nightmare?

She sat up and pulled the covers tight around her shoulders. The house was cold. Maybe she should get up and change. As she had that thought, Matron awoke in her mind and the battle for control started once more.

Rosie was tired, weak, and still vulnerable from her dream. Her body convulsed and shook so hard that she bounced off the bed. As she hit the floor, Matron surged into her mind, and she felt herself slipping.

It was different this time: Matron was stronger, and she was weaker, so she was pushed back further than before. She was in darkness, looking out, but her life was so far away. She was fading inside her own mind, her own body. If this carried on, there would be little of her left, and Matron would win.

I always win, Matron said in her mind, and Rosie blacked out.

CHAPTER 14

The first thing she was aware of was a headache. It was not the splitting pain that she had felt the day before but a dull and persistent ache. Along with the pain, was a deep and overwhelming exhaustion. Rosie didn't want to wake up, so she snuggled down beneath the duvet and turned her back to the window. There was nothing to get up for and another half an hour, or even an hour, really wouldn't matter.

The bed was deliciously comfortable and, despite the pain in her head, she really wanted to sleep. But something was nagging at her mind. Was it that her night clothes felt stiff? Or that her legs ached as well as her head. She wasn't sure, but every time sleep was about to claim her, she was jerked back awake. Maybe she should get up and take a couple of paracetamol. Hunger gnawed at her stomach but she pushed it away. She must not eat. She could make a cup of tea and sit up in bed. That way she was bound to sleep. It always happened. Whenever she had tossed and turned all night, the minute she made herself a drink and was ready to get up, sleep would claim her.

Rosie threw back the duvet and stepped out of bed.

She had taken a few steps before she realized she was wearing jeans and a sweatshirt. Had she been so tired that she forgot to remove them? She pulled back the curtains and the room was flooded with light.

"No!"

Rosie dropped to the floor as she saw that her clothes, her hands, were covered in blood.

For long moments she lay on the floor staring at the crusty blood that covered her hands. What had happened? With a gut-wrenching flash, it all flooded back.

Matron, the house, the previous murder, the nightmare last night and then passing out.

She must have relinquished control to the spirit inside of her and something dreadful had happened.

The urge to scream was overwhelming and she ripped off her clothes, throwing them to the floor as she ran to the bathroom. There in the corner was another pile of bloodied clothes, but the knife was not on it. The knife she had killed Mary with had been moved. Had that knife ripped through more flesh? Had she killed again?

Rosie rushed to the toilet as her throat was filled with vomit. She dropped to the floor and lifted the seat as a hot stream of water and bile poured from her. Again and again she vomited until tears filled her eyes and her throat and chest ached from the effort.

She was naked on the cold floor. Covered in blood, with

THE BATTLE WITHIN

tears running down her cheeks. In a daze, she crawled into the shower and switched on the water. At first it was freezing cold, but she did not move from under the stream. Blood ran from her, swirling down the drain like a red river. Gradually, the water warmed and she scrubbed at her hands, at her arms, and her skin with the back brush. Soon the blood was all gone but she could not stop the scrubbing. She scrubbed until her skin was red and sore and the tears kept falling.

What had happened?

What had she done?

Who had she killed?

Rosie slumped to the floor in the shower and sat there until once again the water ran cold. Still she could not move. Every time she tried to, her stomach flipped and the world spun before her. So she sat and she cried and she hoped that it was all just a terrible dream.

Eventually, Rosie reached up and turned off the water. She stepped from the shower and grabbed a towel, wrapping it around her freezing body.

Then she stumbled from the bathroom and down the stairs. There was one way to find out what she had done. With a shaky hand, she grabbed the television remote and turned it to the news channel.

It came on halfway through the weather and she clicked across to a different channel. It was showing an advert about perfume. It was so flippant and inane that she couldn't watch it and clicked back to the previous channel. The news was just starting. At first it was politics. Some European was spouting doom and gloom. Her mind wasn't listening. It was searching, trying to remember, trying to access Matron's memories without waking her. Then she heard the words she had been dreading to hear.

There had been another murder. This time a man of 62 had been killed as he walked home from the pub. There were no witnesses but the police were appealing for information. They showed a picture of a scruffy looking man with a permanent scowl and a scar over his right eye. His name was Geoffrey and he left behind a wife and two grown children.

Tears were running down Rosie's face and she knew that she was weeping. Only, it was as if it was happening to someone else.

Was she losing control again?

Then her eyes were dragged back to the television. The killer had made a mistake. They had left a necklace. The police described it as a silver chain with a pink crystal rose. They said it was most distinctive and probably very rare and asked that if anyone had any information about such an item that they call a number. The number appeared across the bottom of the screen.

Panic reared in Rosie's chest and her hand flew to her neck. The necklace had been a gift from Amy. Instinctively, she already knew it was missing. It hadn't been there when she showered. Maybe she took it off the night before. Even before she knew she was moving, she was racing toward the stairs. Her feet pounded almost as fast as her heart as she took the stairs two at a time.

If she had taken the necklace off it would be on her dressing table. She searched through her jewelry, searched all the little places she kept her trinkets, but it wasn't there. There was no sign of the necklace and now she knew. Last night she had killed again, only this time she hadn't even known it happened. What could she do? Maybe she should call the police? Maybe she should hand herself in?

In her mind, Matron laughed. *Jail will not keep me. In jail I will have plenty of people to kill, people who can't escape me. I will gain power and then I will simply possess someone else, someone who can free me.*

Rosie had an idea. She stood and opened the door. Through it she could see the hallway. It was clear and bare except for a small table and a vase of everlasting flowers. They looked dusty and faded and she had the urge to throw them down the stairs. Pulling her mind back to the present, she looked at the wall at the other end of the corridor. Was it far enough? Could she get up enough speed?

She kicked off as fast as she could with the intention of smashing her head into that wall. If she went fast enough, then maybe she would die. That way, she would kill herself and Matron would be trapped here.

Before she could get more than a few steps, a vision appeared in her mind. She was dead on the floor. Amy found her. Matron possessed Amy and she was laughing as she left the house.

There was no way out, no way to win.

Her feet slowed and she slumped to the floor in front of the wall. She had lost and there was nothing she could do. This time there was no room for tears, so she just shut down and retreated back into her vault.

* * *

AMY PUSHED a piece of toast around her plate before picking

it up and taking a bite. It was cold and hard, and felt like a rock as it hit her stomach. On the table at her side, her mobile phone sat quiet and innocent and yet it called to her. The pink cover was so bright and she loved it, but today she wished it was something more mundane. Something easier to ignore. The more she thought about the notice in the post office the more ridiculous it seemed, and yet what other explanation was there? Her hand moved toward the phone. She could just look up the leaflet she had taken a picture of and call them to see what they said. Only that just sounded crazy.

All night she had tossed and turned and gone over what had happened. Had she seen something? Could it just have been a cloud passing across the sun and creating shadows in Rosie's house? That was the logical answer, but it didn't seem right. The temperature had dropped, dramatically. It had dropped so low that her breath had misted before her. Was that even possible in a house?

In the corner the radio was playing but she wasn't really listening until the news came on and a murder in Leeds was mentioned.

Her breath caught in her throat and she turned to listen. The more she heard the more terrified she became. A man had been killed. Slaughtered in cold blood, and left on the street. She recognized the area. It was just five minutes' walk from Rosie's house and yet, that could not be.

Then the police were asking for witnesses and asking for information. Amy's blood ran cold as they described an item that had been left near the body. It was a silver chain with a pink crystal rose. She remembered seeing Rosie admire the item and then buying it on the spur of the moment when she found out that Clive was in jail.

The policeman's voice brought her back to the present before she could remember fastening it around Rosie's neck.

The necklace had been found on the body of the victim and the police believed it had been left by the murderer. They didn't understand the meaning of it, and Amy could tell by what they were saying that they didn't think the killer was a woman. They didn't think the killer had lost the necklace but that this necklace had some significance between the killer and his victim. Once more, the man made an appeal for information.

Fear ran through her and she shut out the news bulletin and reached for her phone. Was Rosie killed too? Was she lying somewhere and the police simply hadn't found her yet. Dialing Rosie's number, she waited with her heart pounding. Please Rosie, please be there, please answer.

"Hello," Rosie's voice was flat and disinterested.

"Rosie, I thought you might be..." A cold hand of dread slipped inside her guts and clutched onto her intestines. Something made her stop what she was about to say. She knew she had to be careful, that she had to be clever if she was to survive. Even that thought was crazy, but she changed what she was going to say. "I thought I'd check to see how you were feeling this morning. If you were any better."

"I'm fine, just a bit of a headache so if you don't mind, I want to lie down."

Rosie hung up and Amy let out a groan. There was only one other explanation for the necklace being at the scene. Rosie had been there, Rosie was the killer.

How could she even contemplate that her friend was killing? Rosie couldn't kill a man. It just didn't make sense. It was foolish to think that she had been the only one to buy that necklace. She listened to the news once more and noted down the number to call. Should she ring? Even if only to clear Rosie from the investigation. Surely if she didn't ring, then the shop would. But, she had paid cash, so they have no way of finding her.

It was all too much and she knew that she needed air. Maybe a walk would clear her head and give her time to think. Maybe then she would know what to do. Grabbing her bag, she left the house.

CHAPTER 15

Rosie sat for a long time in the hallway. Nothing mattered, nothing. Not food, or water or anything. It was over three hours later when she eventually got up to use the bathroom. As she did, she saw her laptop and the thought of writing pulled her. It had always been her therapy. Her way of working things out. A coarse laugh rattled around the room and startled her before she realized that she had made it.

So she picked up the laptop and went to the table in the kitchen. Automatically, she set water in the kettle to boil and was soon sat down with a cup of tea. Hunger gnawed at her stomach and she could feel Matron prodding, enquiring what the pain was. She shut it down. Hunger was nothing, she would ignore it.

She opened up her story and began to write. At first it was good to lose her mind in the fictional world. To become her characters and forget everything. Maybe this way she could work out what to do? Maybe she could use her characters to find a way out of this.

Don't be so silly, Matron said inside her head. *There is no way out of this.*

"Shut up," she shouted, and she shut off that part of her mind that held Matron, but it was not easy. Soon, sweat was coursing down her forehead and running down her back. Her arm muscles ached and she looked down to see her fists clenched. Relaxing them, she took in a breath and turned back to her book. Opening a new document, she began to write what had happened as a story.

R was a woman possessed.

M was the antagonist, the evil witch who she needed to defeat.

When plotting, she would then look to see what she could use to solve the problem. What assets did she have, what could she use to win this fight?

For a while, she just let her mind free-write. Usually this was easy for her and lots of thoughts would appear on the screen almost as if by magic. Today, she had hardly anything. The list read:

Amy

Fight

The book

The leaflet

Hunger

Go somewhere remote

Give in, give in, give in, give in, give in, give in, give in, give in, give in, give in give in, give in, give in, give in, give in, give in, give in, give in, give in, give in, give in, give in, give in,

THE BATTLE WITHIN

give in, give in, give in, give in, give in, give in, give in, give in.

Before she could stop herself, three whole pages were filled with those two dreadful words. She slammed the laptop cover down and bit her bottom lip. For a moment, the pain cleared her head and the voice in her mind faded.

It would not last. What could she do?

She reached for her phone and opened a browser. Clicking the microphone, she spoke into the phone, "Find a physic investigator near me."

"The closest physic investigator is The Spirit Guide."

The phone shook in her hand as she squeezed it so tightly her fingers ached. Then she threw it across the room.

You will not be rid of me. Go to sleep.

Rosie felt Matron swarm into her mind and fill her world with pain. She gritted her teeth and bit her lip until blood ran down her chin, but it was no good. She was shaking, convulsing with the effort. As she shook, the chair bounced on the kitchen floor, scraping on the tiles, and then there was just blackness and she was falling. "No, I won't let go," she whispered, just as the world faded from her.

* * *

AMY STEPPED out of the door and was confronted with her Cayenne black Nissan Juke. Seeing the car tore at her heart as she heard Rosie's voice in her head. Heard her laughing as she described the car as an ugly black frog.

It was one of the things they always joked about, one of the things that was always fun between them and she knew

Rosie really liked the car, after all they had chosen it together.

Nothing made sense. This couldn't be Rosie; it couldn't. There was no way she would believe that her friend had killed someone. Even contemplating it was ludicrous. Maybe if she walked for a while and thought this through then it would all begin to make sense?

Decision made, she walked toward the town. She could stop and have a coffee and a muffin for breakfast. Not exactly healthy, but a blood sugar high would probably make it easier to think. Besides, it might just wake her up.

So she cleared her mind and started to walk briskly. Soon the houses gave way to shops and the street grew more crowded. Catching her reflection in a shop window, she ran a hand through her dirty blonde hair. It didn't take long to tease it into the style she liked and it made her feel a little more real, a little more together. Maybe this was just shock and fatigue and she was seeing things that weren't there.

It was just a short walk to the coffee shop but she knew it would be busy this morning. Maybe if she grabbed a paper she could let things go and let her mind work out what was bugging her.

Crossing the busy street, she stepped into the paper shop and picked up the local rag. That was a mistake. The headline spoke of a serial killer in the city and that bloody handprint on Rosie's wall haunted her vision.

"Do you want anything else, miss?" the young man behind the counter asked.

Rosie shook her head and handed over a fiver, waiting for the change. She didn't trust her voice, not at the moment.

Back on the street, she turned to her right and there was the post office. Though she wanted to walk straight past, she was pulled to the noticeboard. It was gone. The card she had seen and taken a picture of last night was no longer there.

Was that a sign?

She couldn't stop a laugh that sounded a little hysterical. Here she was, the most unlikely person to believe in signs, ghosts, messages from beyond, most definitely UFOs, and she was jumping at the slightest little thing. While she stared at the window, a hand reached in and placed another card.

She wanted to turn and walk away and to not look at it, but she couldn't. It was as if she was rooted to the spot. Her hands were sweating, her fingers shaking, and she was breathing so fast she was close to hyperventilating. How could she even contemplate this ridiculous idea?

The hand pulled away and she read the card.

Do you have something strange and unusual in your life?
Something so bizarre that it doesn't seem real?
You are not alone, we can help.
Contact Jesse and Gail at The Spirt Guide
Your local supernatural and paranormal detective agency.

WITH SHAKING FINGERS, she pulled out her phone and snapped a picture of the card. Then suddenly angry, she turned and stormed away. This just didn't make sense. It couldn't be a ghost, it just couldn't. Such things didn't exist and even if they did, why would they go after poor Rosie. It was a much more sensible conclusion that her friend had suffered a nervous breakdown. Maybe Amy should call the doctor, or the police. Once more her hands were in her hair, only this time they weren't smoothing it. She had the urge to yank it out and scream at the unfairness of the situation.

Taking a deep breath, she walked into the coffee shop and joined the queue.

It took a good 10 minutes to get served and by then Amy was hungry, grumpy, and so ambivalent about what to do that she was rocking from one extreme to the other. One moment she wanted to ring that number and demand to see them now. Then she wanted to call the police and tell them about the necklace. But, what would that do to Rosie, especially if she was innocent? It didn't bear thinking about.

At last a woman handed over her coffee, which had taken over three minutes to make and tasted exactly the same as the one out of the instant machine. Grabbing her tray, she surveyed the café. It was busy, but right along the back corner there were a couple of small tables free. Heading over to one of them, she sat down and took a big sip of the hot, strong brew.

It warmed her gullet and chased away some of the chill she was still feeling. It warmed up the cold empty spot inside that knew something was terribly wrong. Though she brought the paper, she couldn't bear to look at it, and folded it over so only the sports pages were showing.

Then she went through everything that had happened... one by one. From picking Rosie up at RedRise House, she had immediately known something was wrong. Rosie had looked terrible and she had smelt even worse. It was as if she hadn't bathed in days, and that was not like her. Amy put it down to stress and maybe the possibility that the house had no facilities. Maybe that's why she had left so suddenly.

Or had something happened there? Had that been the start of all of this?

Then she remembered how cold Rosie was when she took her home. How she snapped all the time and didn't want to talk, and then how she almost pushed her out of her house. Next, she had heard her talking to herself and talking about killing. The two different voices, the blood on the wall. The superior demeanor she had developed, and then the two most terrible pieces of evidence. The first was the shadow she had seen twice. Was there any way she could have imagined that? No matter how she tried to believe she hadn't really seen something, she couldn't forget it and how it made her feel. Something had been in the kitchen… something cold, something wrong, something dark.

The second and worst piece of evidence was the necklace. She knew if she went to see Rosie that she wouldn't be wearing it. One way or another, the necklace she had bought her friend had been found on a murder victim.

The muffin sat untouched in front of her but she picked up the coffee and took a long drink. It helped, even if only a little. She had to do this, so she picked up the phone and dialed a number.

"Hello, Jesse speaking."

At first, Amy froze. She didn't know why she had rung and she didn't know what she was going to say. For a moment she almost hung up.

"I understand that you are confused and scared," a soft male voice came over the phone. "We can help you. But even if we can't, what have you got to lose?"

Silence ticked down the line, but she didn't hang up.

"I'm not saying whatever you're going through is supernatural; it might not be. That is a big part of our job, sorting out what is supernatural and explaining what isn't. Why not let us come and talk to you and listen to what is happening? We will give you impartial advice and we can help you."

"My name is Amy and I'm at the coffee shop on the High Street. When can you come to see me?"

"Hi, Amy. We can set off straight away and be with you within the hour. How would I recognize you?"

"I... I don't know whether this is such a good idea."

"We will come along and just have a chat. If you don't like what we say, then that's no problem. Maybe just talking to someone else will help you think things through and put them into perspective. My name is Jesse and I've got short brown hair my wife's Gail; she has a brunette bob. Whereabouts are you seated and what do you look like?"

His voice was so gentle and so ordinary. He seemed to be saying that this was not supernatural and that he could tell her what was happening. Before she knew it, she was describing herself and telling him where she was sitting, and then before he could say another word, she hung up.

Now she just had to wait until these two crazy people came to see her. As the minutes passed, she began to believe that they must be con artists and she wanted to get up and walk out. But, she couldn't. She owed it to Rosie to at least try and work this out.

CHAPTER 16

*J*esse steered the old Jeep along the winding country roads toward Leeds. It was a trip that was now quite familiar to him and no longer required his full attention. The countryside was stark, but beautiful. The road sloped away to the left and rose above them on the right. It was dotted with the occasional tree, lots of sheep, and the dry stonewalling that was so prevalent on the moors.

For the last few weeks they have been very busy, but of the five cases they had dealt with, only one had been a genuine haunting. Of the others, one had been the case of, so-called friends, trying to scare the client. The others were easily explained by rattling pipes and faulty boilers. It was amazing how much central heating pipes would rattle and knock if there was air in the system. Even to professionals like Gail and Jesse, it could be quite scary.

The last case he had dealt with, the family were convinced that they had a ghost. They had even communicated with it by getting it to answer the questions with knocks. They had heard it walking across the floor and there were cold spots and drops in temperature, which seemed to point toward a spirit.

It had taken both Jesse and Gail a while to persuade them that there was nothing supernatural there. Bleeding the central heating system and then calling a plumber in to do a power flush certainly helped. Jesse had then found himself lifting floorboards and padding the pipework. Eventually though, he had been able to put the client's mind at rest and move on.

To Gail, it had been disappointing and frustrating. She was still so excited about communicating with spirits, that the more mundane side of the business didn't interest her. But to Jesse, it was all part of the job. Putting someone's mind at ease, relieving their fear, was just as important whether it was a ghost or not.

They had been so busy that so far they haven't had a night to themselves in the last month and a half.

Gail was still working her job as an architect and because they had been so busy during the day, she was often working at night. So far, even though their paranormal investigations agency was going well, she wasn't prepared to give up her job and Jesse couldn't blame her. It also meant he hadn't had time to propose. He wanted to do it properly, romantically, or maybe he was just procrastinating.

The ring was still in his desk drawer and every so often, when she wasn't there, he would get it out and look at it. Maybe he should take her away for a few days. Book a short break and go, no matter what came up.

Yeah, he would do that. After this job he would clear some time and take her away. They could go back to London for a few days. Take in a show, do some shopping, he could book a nice restaurant, and there he could propose. Just thinking about it put a big smile on his face and he decided that was the plan. As soon as this job was finished, he would book it and no matter what came up, they would go away.

"What are you smiling at?" Gail asked.

Jesse felt heat hit his cheeks and he kept his eyes on the road. He was sure she knew what he was planning, as she always seemed to be teasing him whenever he was thinking about it.

"I was just thinking what a fabulous job we have," he said, keeping his eyes on the road.

"What do you think about this one? Do you think it is genuine? Is there anything I ought to know before we go in there?"

Jesse thought about it for a few moments. Gail was very good at putting people at ease, much better than he was. Her only problem was she didn't have much patience and if she thought it wasn't a real haunting, sometimes she thought the client was wasting their time. It was all part of learning the business. Understanding that the client was frightened and that the fear was real, even if the haunting wasn't.

"She didn't tell me much, but I can tell that she is afraid for her friend. I think this one we just play by ear, feel things out, and see how we go."

Gail nodded. "This coffee shop is becoming like a second office for us. If you are not careful, they'll be charging us rent."

Jesse laughed and steered the car into the car park.

"Okay, let's go meet our new client." Saying that still gave him a special sort of buzz.

The coffee shop was crowded, but they spotted the client quite quickly. She was sitting at a small table on the right near the back. She was the only person alone and looked as if it was taking all her effort to stay still. It was as if she wanted to leave and was forcing herself to sit there.

Jesse and Gail threaded their way through the crowd and walked up to the table. Jesse held out his hand. "Hi Amy, I'm Jesse and this is Gail. It's really nice to meet you. Would you like another drink?"

Amy stood and shook his hand. She was an attractive looking girl, her dirty blonde bed hair styled short. Her big brown eyes were worried and the lines beneath them told of her fatigue. Gail squeezed her hand as they shook and gave her a slight smile.

While Jesse got the drinks, Gail sat down. He knew that she would develop a rapport easier without him there.

Gail was the one with the talent now as she could sense spirits much easier than Jesse, but he doubted she would sense anything here. They would have to meet the friend, if they determined it was worthwhile.

Jesse put the three drinks on the table and sat down.

"Now, tell us everything," he said.

"I don't know where to start." Amy's eyes were moist with unshed tears and she looked down, a little ashamed.

"I understand that this is frightening and difficult. When was the first time you noticed your friend was different?" Jesse knew it was easier to go right back to the beginning. That way, what Amy was telling them wouldn't sound quite as strange. They could gain her confidence and get a feeling for whether this was a real haunting before she had to tell them anything too difficult.

Amy looked up and chewed on her lip for a moment, then she nodded. "I house sit for a living. Rosie had a really bad... she was attacked by her boyfriend and beaten very badly. If I hadn't found her she would have died. He disappeared, and she ended up living in hotels to hide from him for some time. I suggested that she take on a housesitting job in order to get away. To somewhere where he couldn't find her, and to give her a chance to write in peace. I forgot to say she writes for a living." She stopped and sipped at her coffee.

"Go on," Jesse encouraged.

"I got her this job at a lovely old remote house. I thought it would be perfect for her, but when I went to stay with her for a few days, she wanted to come back and she was acting really strange."

"Strange, how?" Jesse asked.

Amy looked up at her, her eyes narrowed. It looked like she didn't want to say.

"You can tell us. It doesn't matter how strange it sounds," Gail said.

Amy nodded, but a few moments passed before she was able to form the words. "The first thing I noticed was... she was dirty and she smelt really bad. It looked like she hadn't washed in days, and that isn't like Rosie. Then she was cold and distant, and at times she didn't seem to understand things." Amy's mouth fell open, her eyes widened.

"Oh my God. Maybe she's had a stroke or something. Oh my

God, what am I doing talking to you when she could be sick or dying?"

"Don't worry, we will rule out a medical condition if we think we need to. Now where was this house?" Jesse asked.

"It was right out in the sticks the other side of Leeds; it's called RedRise House."

Jesse felt the old excitement curl in his stomach. RedRise House was not too far away and it had a reputation. There were tales of people going missing there in the past and he had heard that it had once been used for occult rituals. It was one of the properties that they planned to investigate but, as always, they hadn't had time just yet.

"We have heard of RedRise House; it has some history," Gail said.

Jesse touched her foot beneath the table, his signal to leave this to him. When they were investigating, it was best not to cloud the client's view with any tales. It was amazing how much evidence the human mind could find to support something that it thought was true. However, knowing that Rosie had been to RedRise House certainly made things very interesting.

"What else did you notice?" Jesse asked.

"She was cruel at times and her face would look as if she was trying to stop herself from saying something. It was like she was trying to stop an expression from showing. At first I thought it was a joke, and then one day I was outside her house and I heard her talking to herself in two different voices. She was talking about... oh, God, I don't know whether to tell you this?"

Gail reached out and took her hand.

"It's okay," Jesse said. "Whatever you say will be in confidence and we will help you through this, no matter what it is."

"She was talking about killing someone. It was as if she was arguing with herself."

Jesse nodded. He really wanted to meet Rosie and to investigate this place. So far, he could think of two main reasons this could be happening: The first was that she had suffered a schizophrenic breakdown, and the other was that she was possessed. He believed it was the latter.

"Could she have done this? Could she be mad?"

"It's possible, but this sounds a little like a possession to me. Spirits are often not bothered about cleanliness. They also take time to fully control a person. During that time, they will be fighting the host they are within and they don't know everything the host knows. That would make your friends behavior strange. I think we need to meet her... would that be possible?"

"There is something else, something really bad, but I can't tell you," Amy said.

Jesse looked down at the local paper next to Amy. He knew what the headline was, and his excitement turned to fear. Could this haunting have anything to do with the murders that were taking place? It was a lot to infer, but his gut said *yes*.

"Anything you tell us will be in confidence. We would never report your friend, and even if we did, who would believe us?"

Amy looked up at him and he could see that she wanted to talk, but she was scared.

"Do you believe she has hurt someone?" he asked the question in his softest voice and he felt Gail come to attention next to him.

Amy nodded.

"Then you must be even more careful. Do not go see your friend. If she won't come to meet us, then we will visit her. We will find a way to stop this and to help your friend."

Amy smiled and it lit up her face. "I can try and get her to come for lunch tomorrow. There's a little cafe across the road, can you make that?"

"Yeah, that would be great, say 1 p.m.?"

"Yes. I will get her there one way or another. Thank you. Now, do I pay you?" Amy looked embarrassed.

"Let's see your friend first," Jesse said. "Be careful. If she is possessed, she will likely want to sever relations with you, and that could be dangerous. Try and arrange things over the phone and if you go see her, don't push it."

"Okay," Amy said, but the color had dropped from her face and once more her eyes shone with tears.

CHAPTER 17

Rosie was walking down a dark street. The sound of her heels echoed on the houses around her and each step caused a sharp pain in her temple. How had she gotten there?

You're just my passenger, Matron's words echoed inside her head. *From now on, you go where I want, you do what I want, and you kill who I want.*

"No, no I won't," Rosie shouted the words, but her mouth didn't move and they sounded insipid inside her own head.

Everything was fuzzy, from her vision to the way her body felt. It was all disconnected, all out of control. She was losing this battle, she was fading inside herself. If she didn't do something soon there would be nothing of her left. But what could she do? How could she take back control?

You can't. I have two now. Two acolytes and soon there will be three. Then I will have Amy and you will do nothing to stop me.

Inside her own head, Rosie screamed and shouted, but not a word of it came out.

They turned left onto another street and carried on walking. Rosie knew what she was doing. Matron looking for somebody alone, someone vulnerable. She was looking for another easy kill.

How could she stop her?

You can't.

"I can and I will."

Rosie's mind was filled with pain... searing, boiling, excruciating pain that made her retreat back inside herself. She drew back into her vault... back to safety.

The pain eased and she was able to breathe again. Cautiously she peeked out of her vault and watched what was going on.

Matron had walked for maybe half an hour during the time it took Rosie to recover, yet it had felt like mere minutes. She had to be careful, cleverer than this if she was going to win.

Her body's heartbeat kicked up a notch and she could feel Matron's excitement. There, across the street, was a young man. He was maybe twenty-one or two and he was very drunk. Stumbling along the street, he tripped on a raised paving stone before stumbling into the wall. Then he laughed and slid down to the ground. Having tried to get up a couple of times but failing, he slumped back down and laughed some more.

Matron crossed the road, looking left and right. Not for traffic. This was a quiet part of town. No, she was looking for witnesses.

Rosie bided her time, waiting for any chance to save the man.

THE BATTLE WITHIN

Her heart, Matron's heart, was racing now as they got closer to their prey.

Sprawled on the street, the young man pushed a lock of floppy coal black hair out of his eyes and looked around. He was embarrassed and trying to see if he was being watched.

Matron froze, slinking back into the shadows of one of the trees that lined the street.

The young guy continued to scan his surroundings. There was a bemused expression on his face as he stared around him. Seeing no one there, he tried to haul himself up to his feet.

As he did, Matron stepped out from the tree and walked to the next one. Rosie felt her excitement build… she was so sure she could do this. Rosie knew she had to stop her, but how?

Floppy-haired man was half standing now, leaning against the wall with his back to them. There was a little over 10 feet between them and Rosie was aware of the knife in her hand.

Where had it come from?

Had it been there all along?

She didn't know the answer, but there wasn't time to work that out right now. Fighting back the revulsion at the wet leather in her fingers, she steeled herself to act and bided her time.

The man was standing, wobbling on his feet and still clutching onto the wall.

Matron crept along behind him. Intending to get within striking distance before he even knew she was there. The street was dark and tree-lined and they were between streetlamps. The shadows were in her favor as was the inebriated state of her intended victim.

With all the concentration she could muster, Rosie slammed down her left leg. The sound of it slapping onto the pavement echoed in the street, and the young man jumped into the air and turned around quite comically.

He was staring right at them. Rosie could feel Matron's anger, followed by a burst of pain. It wouldn't stop her, not this time as she was becoming immune to it. Before Matron could act, she opened her mouth and screamed, "Run, she wants to kill you! She has a knife! Run quickly!"

Rosie had expected pain but instead she felt confusion. Suddenly, Matron lurched forward with the knife in her right hand. Rosie had no control as her arm raised high into the air. Poised now for the killer blow.

The drunken man could hardly see through his floppy black hair, but there was a jovial smile on his face. He expected this was just a joke. Possibly even thought one of his mates had put her up to it. Then he saw the knife and his drunken expression became one of stone-cold sobriety. Moving backward with surprising speed, he seemed to have a chance. Then his feet caught on each other and he was sent sprawling to the pavement. The look on his face was one of abject fear as the knife in Rosie's hand plunged toward him.

Matron moved so fast. Jumping across the distance and pouncing on him like a lion on its prey. She didn't bother with the ritual tonight and didn't bother which way she was facing. She simply slashed the blade through his jugular as Rosie screamed in despair, watching the confusion on his terrorized face. The word *why* on his lips as the light went out of his eyes.

* * *

Rosie woke in her bed. This time there was no blissful ignorance. No period of not knowing what had happened. She could even feel the dried blood on her clothes and the memory of what had happened was ever so clear. However, once more, she was in control again. Each time Matron killed she gained power and yet it seemed that just after the killing, she was at her weakest. How could she use that to her advantage?

Throwing back the covers, she was aghast to see the bloodstains on the bed. How many times had she gone to sleep with her blood-covered clothes on?

Quickly stripping off her clothes, she walked through to the bathroom. On the floor in the corner was now three days' worth of blood-soaked clothing. Her stomach began to wretch a dry heave at the ghastly and all-too-familiar sight. Climbing into the shower, she began to wash her body clean. Once more, the water ran red as she soaked and shampooed and scrubbed at herself.

Today she wasn't going to worry about what was done. She pushed away the feeling of disgust and despair. She forced back the guilt. It was time to concentrate on the future and how to stop this madness. Maybe she had a little time. Maybe she could talk to Amy before Matron regained control.

Showered and changed, she walked down the stairs, hunger and fatigue making her dizzy as she grabbed the phone. The temperature in the kitchen dropped and yet she wasn't scared. Maybe she should be as she knew what was about to happen. Mary would appear to her from out of the mist. Mary believed she had killed her and no doubt wanted revenge, yet she didn't care. If the old ghost killed her, then maybe this nightmare would be over.

As she watched, in the corner of the kitchen a darkness began to form. It was like a dark mist, like smoke. It swirled and coalesced before her. Moving, forming, and then disappearing as quickly as it came.

"Don't go. Please don't leave me. I need your help."

As she said the words, a groan came from behind her. It was a keening of pain and fear, and she turned around to see a man of about sixty. There was a scar over his right eye and his face was distorted into a grimace of agony.

Rosie let out a scream and jumped back as the hair rose on her arms. She hadn't expected a man.

Then he was gone.

With her hand on her chest she waited, spinning around in the room. Who was the man? He had to be the other life Matron had taken?

Now I have two, she had said, *and soon there will be three.*

The mist was back… it rushed toward her and fear forced her to move back, but the mist stopped and reformed, and she could see Mary within its smoky tendrils. The old woman was smiling, reaching out with her thin bird-like hands.

Rosie had the need to take her hand, so she reached out. Her fingers traced through the older woman, there was nothing there, just a sense of cold.

Mary looked confused, worried. The shrill tone of a phone sounded and the mist was gone.

THE BATTLE WITHIN

Rosie picked up the phone.

"Hey Rosie, how are you?" Amy sounded jovial, but she could hear that her friend was worried, afraid of what she was saying and of what she would hear in return.

"I'm okay at the moment. I can't say much but I need you to understand that I am dangerous." A spike of pain lanced through her brain, but then it was gone. "Did you put that card in the post office window and did you see another advert there?"

There was silence on the end of the phone. As it dragged between them she could feel Matron waking. The old woman knew she was in danger and she was starting to come forth. Rosie didn't have long. If she didn't act now she would lose control.

"I have to tell you..." The words stopped in her throat and Matron filled her head with molten lava. The heat spread and melted her thoughts away.

Rosie pulled back into her vault to avoid the pain but she had to try and look out. As she did, the pain was gone. The shadowy mist was back in front of her and she could see Mary smiling within it. She was holding the hands of the scarred man and the floppy-haired drunk. Rosie whispered, *sorry* to them and looked for the phone. It was on the floor.

Picking it up, she said, "I'm sorry Amy I don't have long and I can't say what I want to say."

"I understand. I have a possible buyer for your computer. Can you meet me at the little cafe near the post office tomorrow for lunch, around one p.m.? If we can sell your computer, a lot of your problems will be solved."

"I will be there, thank you so much and I love you."

Mary smiled and the smoke dissolved.

Matron was back.

What was that?

Rosie filled her mind with fear for Amy and in doing so feared going to lunch. Who cared if she sold her computer? She had to keep away from Amy. She must keep her friend safe. Then, Matron coursed into her mind and Rosie pulled back into her vault. She had to stay there and keep her thoughts to herself, just until after the meeting.

The smug feeling that came over Matron was enough. The woman thought she was in control. Rosie just hoped that she wasn't. She also had hope that Amy understood and that she would receive the help she so desperately needed to stop this evil bitch.

CHAPTER 18

Rosie awakened on the kitchen floor. She was stiff and achy and the fuzzy feeling was back. *Where was Matron?*

I am here, the guttural voice said in her head. *We need to be going to lunch.*

"Never!" Rosie shouted. "We will stay in this house forever. You will never get near Amy."

Rosie was aware of a necklace around her neck. It was heavy. She glanced down and it was the pentagram that she remembered bringing from RedRise House.

"Appear," the words came out of her mouth, and she felt a charge in the air. The black mist formed and swirled, giving her a sense of hope. If Mary was coming back, then she would have help—but Matron was pleased; she wanted this.

The mist formed and three figures emerged from it. Mary was there, translucent, her pink coat, now gray, and she wasn't smiling. Her face was contorted, and she appeared to be—afraid. Next to her was the drunken man. His floppy black hair covered one side of his face and fell over his right eye, but the terror in his left was truly apparent. On her left, the scarred man came into view. He was less visible, almost totally opaque, but the scowl on his face was quite apparent and the look in his eyes sent a chill down her back. These spirits were no longer her friends, no longer on her side. It looked like Matron finally had her power base.

You will bow before me, Matron said.

The figures swirled and were gone for a moment. Matron grabbed hold of the necklace in her right hand and with her left, she appeared to grab onto the air and pull it toward her. The spirits were back, and this time they looked defeated, even Mary. They were wearing long black hooded cloaks and they bowed to her.

Rosie's vision shimmered as if she were looking through tinted glass. She was fading. She tried to move her hands, her legs, to no avail. There was no sensation, no connection, nothing. Fear filled her. Was it too late? Had she already lost this battle?

Tears formed in her eyes… or did they?

"No, you are just my host now… just my prisoner. I will show you what I want, and one day even you will bow down to me in all my greatness."

Rosie wept inside her prison, tears that would never fall. It filled her mind with one thought: keeping Amy safe.

The smug satisfaction she felt emanating from Matron was both terrifying and gratifying.

* * *

Jesse and Gail walked into the cafe. It was the exact opposite of the coffee shop. Whereas that was all white with straight edges and shiny plastic, this was rustic, having round tables and mismatched chairs. Each of the tables had a red checkered tablecloth and a little bunch of silk flowers. Behind the counter, a woman in her mid-fifties smiled warmly at them.

They ordered two teas and chose the table in the window. It had the largest gap around it and would give them some privacy.

Gail looked around the room. There were only three other tables occupied. Two with elderly couples and one with a woman and her three young kids. They were well-behaved and tucked into their food with gusto.

"This place is all right," Jesse said.

"Let's see what the tea tastes like first." Gail's eyebrows rose and she smiled at him.

Neither of them was interested in the drink. They were too excited about what would happen and how they would handle this.

Jesse adjusted his chair so he could look at the door without staring. This was an exciting case and he knew there was something more, something that Amy was holding back. He felt it in his bones and she had alluded to as much.

"We have to get her to open up," he said.

"I will do my best, but she's scared."

"I know."

The owner came over with a tray holding a large china teapot in white with a pretty pink rose design. There were two china cups with saucers, a sugar bowl, and a milk jug that all matched.

"Wow," Jesse said as he watched Gail's eyes light up with delight. She loved her tea, and this was something special.

They thanked the lady and Gail poured the tea -Jesse's first, adding milk. Then she let the pot brew for a while as she twiddled with her fingers.

"Are they late yet?"

Jesse shook his head. "No we were early. Do you remember our sign?"

Gail poured her tea and took a sip, nodding her appreciation.

"Yes. I tap my right thumb on the table if I sense a spirit."

Jesse smiled. It had been foolish of him to ask, but he was nervous about this one.

They drank in silence, both wanting to ask questions, but both trying to think of the right words to use with their client. It would be a difficult conversation and they would simply have to play it by ear… that was if Amy and her friend Rosie even turned up.

"They're not coming, are they?" Gail asked as the minutes ticked past so very slowly.

"It's possible." Jesse smiled. This was a part of the job and would be something Gail would have to get used to. It was frustrating and disheartening at times, but people lost their nerve, or the haunting stopped. Of course, there were also the times when the whole thing had been a con, a set-up, a joke at their expense. He didn't think this was one of those cases. He had a gut feeling about this one and he knew it was going to be bad.

As if on cue, Amy came through the cafe door. Her hair was even more untamed than normal and she was wearing no makeup. She looked around and spotted them before looking around the tables once more. Disappointment crossed her face as she came over.

"Hi Amy," Gail said, and she jumped up and pulled her into her arms.

It was such a sweet gesture and he could see Amy wanted to pull Gail to her and hold her for longer, despite the fact that they hardly knew each other. It was Gail's skill and he loved her for it.

"Hi Amy," Jesse said and watched as she looked at the door and searched the tables once more. "Don't worry if she is late or even if she doesn't turn up. We can talk and find out more and if necessary, we will visit her."

Amy smiled and sat down in a chair opposite them.

"Can I get you anything?"

Amy jumped to see the cafe owner standing there with her notepad.

"Oh, I'm so sorry my dear," she said.

"Just a coffee, please."

Once they were alone again she seemed to slump into her seat. "I am so worried about Rosie, so terribly worried."

Jesse kicked Gail's leg warning her to keep quiet. He wanted to leave some silence. To give Amy the courage to tell them what she wanted to tell them. But then the door to the cafe opened again and a young woman came in. Jesse would imagine she was in her mid-thirties but knew from what Amy had said that she wasn't quite thirty. The possession, if that's what it was, had aged her. Her long brunette hair was loose around her shoulders but matted to the side of her head. It looked as if it hadn't been brushed in days.

Whereas Amy's bed hair was usually carefully done and fashionable, this just spoke of sloth. As she came over, they could see a scar across her left cheek. It didn't look as bad as he expected. A feeling of sympathy came over him. Rosie had been through so much.

He pushed it away. He had to deal with this emotionlessly and take the best route for all involved. She was wearing an old sweatshirt in a light blue which was stained down the front and dirty looking jeans.

She walked toward the table with her back straight and her head up. It made her look even stranger. That she would be so proud of herself wearing such dirty clothes was almost laughable. Or it would have been if it didn't' point to her being possessed?

She came straight to the table and stood before them. Jesse knew she expected reverence. It was written on her face and so he decided to give it to her. He stood and bowed before her.

"Welcome, it is such an honor to have you here. We are so pleased to meet you. He rushed around and pulled out a chair. At the same time he felt with every nerve of his body, but he couldn't discern anything. He cursed his lack of talent and looked at Gail.

She was sensitive and he imagined he could see her hair rising with static. Her expression was closed, a little too closed, and her right thumb tapped frantically on the table, she most definitely felt something.

CHAPTER 19

Matron was pleased with the café when she walked in. It looked a little familiar. A little more like a tea room than she had expected.

Over to one side, near to the window, Amy sat with two people. These must be the buyers for the computer, whatever that was. It didn't matter. All she intended from this meeting was to ingratiate herself with Amy. She would work it so that she could get Amy alone and back to her house. Now she had three acolytes, she had enough strength to keep Rosie from influencing her own body for long enough to kill Amy.

Once that deed was done, Rosie would be broken and she would be hers forever. A smile came across her face as she got to the table.

Amy sat on the side closest to the window and opposite her was a man with hair so short you could see through it to his scalp. It was most inappropriate. He was seated next to a woman with shoulder-length brown hair and a nondescript face. And yet there was something about her that drew Matron's eye. *What was it?*

Before Matron could analyze it further, the man stood and bowed. Did he recognize her? Understand her power? Maybe he felt it. Before long, many would feel it and she would use that to build her souls and to increase her influence even further. She would have this town as her own. She would make them all bow before her, and Rosie would watch. It was a delicious thought and she almost gave Rosie some access, but that was dangerous. Her souls were all tied to the property, to her altar, and she was not as strong without them. If she let Rosie out, there was a possibility that she would cause trouble.

The man kept his eyes lowered as he pulled out her chair. Matron sat down and allowed him to move it in for her. As he did their hands almost touched. A trickle of electricity ran up her arm and into her chest. This one had power, but he couldn't access it. He was blocked.

Inside Matron the slight shock woke Rosie. She was deep inside her vault, no longer hiding out of choice but because she had none. If she came out, then Matron would still be in control, but she sensed that something was different so she peeked out to see the café.

It was a place which held good memories. She had visited it, as well as the modern coffee shop on many occasions with Amy. They came here if they wanted to eat and to the coffee shop for just a drink.

Seated at the table were a couple and Amy. Her friend looked stressed, tired, and frankly scared. She wanted to reach out and hug her. To tell her everything would be all right.

It won't be, soon she will belong to me, the voice was harsh in her mind. Gloating and as always smug and superior.

Rosie shrank back a little as if she was hurt by the comment, but she stayed there to watch. The man had his head bowed and he looked as if he was under Matron's control. Was that possible?

Soon all who come near me will feel my power, Matron said.

The woman looked worried but also strangely confident. Was she the one who had come to buy her computer? She used the same phrase that she had used all along, forcing her mind to think that was why they were here. That way, Matron would not be warned by any stray thoughts. After all, she really wanted to sell this computer.

Matron pushed her away in her mind and looked across at Amy. "How are you, my friend?" she asked, and Rosie felt her lips pull into a sneer. Was it meant to be a smile?

She could see from Amy's reaction that she was not fooled, but still Amy smiled back.

"I'm good and I see you are looking so much better. How is your novel coming along?"

Matron balked and searched Rosie's memories. Rosie fought a little but soon gave in and let her see the plot. Let her know that it was not really going anywhere at the moment and that she needed to sell the computer to move the novel forward. The words made no sense but she knew Amy would understand that. It was as much of a code as she could manage.

"I'm a little stuck at the moment, until we sell this com-puter. I expect you to arrange that for me."

"Well that's why we're here," Amy said, and this time her smile was genuine as she pointed to Gail and Jesse.

* * *

Jesse sat back down and beneath the table he squeezed Gail's hand. It gave her strength and built her confidence. Though it was terrifyingly strange to be here, she knew that she had to do this. Jesse had felt the newcomer's power. She was sure of that, but he couldn't see what she could see. The woman before her buzzed with power and was surrounded by darkness. But that wasn't what turned her stomach to mush and made her knees shake.

As Rosie walked into the café she could see her terror beneath the fake smile. But there was more than that. She could see the face of the spirit that possessed her. It was like a faint impression behind Rosie's real face, and it was evil. It had a long crooked nose, cold black eyes, and skeletal cheekbones. There was a smugness about the being and the more she saw of it, the more afraid she was. Somehow she knew that it was ancient and powerful. As she turned her eyes on her, Gail drew in a breath and the air buzzed between them. The hair on her arms rose and her stomach tightened into a knot of fear.

Then she saw a glimpse of the real Rosie beneath the façade. The woman was afraid but fighting, and there was a glimmer of hope in her eyes. As Amy spoke about selling the computer she understood that Rosie was fighting, and clever. One way or another she would help her.

Jesse had explained that to get rid of this spirit would require a full exorcism and that it could be painful and traumatic to all of them. He wanted to get Rosie back to her house and to

THE BATTLE WITHIN

deal with it alone. Without Amy there, Gail couldn't see that happening. Amy was scared, but she was fiercely protective of her friend and she wouldn't leave willingly.

"So, Rosie, tell me all about this computer. Why do you want rid of it?" Gail watched the confusion cross the spirit's face as she asked the question, but Rosie remained calm.

It was so strange looking at the woman across from her. Gail could see three faces. The one that everyone could see was bad enough. Often confused, often displaying contradictory expressions, she looked like some comedian contorting her face to gain a laugh, but no one found this funny. For a moment, Gail thought of Phil Cool known as the rubber-faced man, and it briefly broke her fear.

Beneath the external face she could see the battle between Rosie and the spirit. Old Hag, came into her mind and she wondered where it had come from. Maybe it was relevant or maybe it was just the face that made her think that.

Giving a gentle smile she tried to encourage Rosie, to let her know that she understood and that she was on her side. It was impossible to tell if she saw or understood the gesture because she was pushed backward and her image faded.

A rush of dread filled Gail's veins with ice. Rosie didn't have long. How she knew that, she wasn't sure, but something told her that if they didn't free her soon that Rosie would be irreparably damaged.

The spirit still looked confused and Gail repeated the question. "Why are you selling the computer?" As she waited for an answer she tried to draw in a breath. The air was cold and there was a pressure on her chest that squeezed her lungs like a bellows. Was the spirit doing this?

For a moment there was confusion before them, and then Rosie surfaced once more. Maybe the spirit needed to bring her back to answer such questions. Then she was gone again, yanked back inside her skull.

"I don't think it suits my lifestyle," the spirit said.

"I understand, and I think we're interested. May we come and see it?" Gail wanted to reach out and touch her hand, to give Rosie some comfort, and to see if she could feel anything else. She inched her hands closer to those of Rosie, which were folded before her on the table. As she looked at them she saw that they were old, thin, with swollen and crippled knuckles.

Rosie shook before them as the spirit fought for control then she gave a terrible smile. It was all teeth and no eyes and it made Gail jerk her hands. As she did their fingers touched for just a fraction of a second.

The air crackled, and Gail felt such terrible cold and despair. A gasp escaped her throat.

The spirit was standing. The face beneath the face was afraid. The smile was replaced with a snarl and she turned to go.

"Rosie, what is it?" Amy shouted.

Gail wanted to reach out and grab her. To pull her back to the table, but she couldn't do it, not here, not in front of people. They were losing her, and if she left then she was sure Rosie would be lost.

"I really want to see your computer," she said in desperation, and started to stand.

Jesse put a hand on her shoulder and held her there. "If she flees, then let her go," he whispered.

"I changed my mind," the spirit said. "Amy come and have a coffee with me, please. I demand your company."

Rosie's body turned and raced from the café, but Gail saw her frightened face lingering before them for long seconds after she had gone.

Amy stood, about to follow. Her mouth was open and there were tears in her eyes. Jesse grabbed hold of her and pulled her back down.

As the café door closed, Gail felt as if the room was suddenly brighter and she drew in a big breath.

CHAPTER 20

Moments before.

The conversation continued and fear filled Rosie's mind as Matron forced her back. The spirit was so strong, even without her acolytes. The last thing she saw was Amy smile, and she could swear that the smile was meant for her. Pulling back, she rushed into her vault and slammed the door. Normally she would have stayed there for a long while. She would listen if she could and rebuild her strength, but time was short.

Already she had so little free will, and soon it would be gone forever. Taking a metaphoric breath, she steeled herself and pushed with all she had.

Matron fought back and squealed inside her mind. The sound was loud and painful. It made her feel as if her eardrums had burst, and she imagined she could feel blood running down her cheeks. But it worked. She peeked out and saw Amy and the new couple. They had power, but Matron

THE BATTLE WITHIN

knew. How could she help them? How could she explain what they had to do?

Her body began to shake as Matron fought for control. She could see by the look on Amy's face that she could see through the façade Matron had built.

Rosie fought harder than she had ever fought in her life. Her body ached and convulsed and shook. Her teeth rattled in her skull and she could feel the ice cold as the spirit fought to remain in control.

Her face contorted into a terrible grimace that was meant to be a smile, and she felt pushed back by pain and sheer strength.

But Gail jerked her hands as the battle continued, and it touched her fingers. Rosie felt it. A real touch; not the second-hand feeling she had been getting while Matron was in control.

The air crackled between them and Gail let out a gasp.

She had felt her, she understood. Maybe not everything but something. Rosie withdrew before Matron could read her mind. She feigned panic and drew back as quickly as she could. Once inside her vault she slammed the door and collapsed inside her own mind. The pain still permeated every fiber of her being, but the horror was starting to fade. For the first time in a long while she had hope.

* * *

Moments before.

Matron could tell that the couple before her had power. It

reverberated around them. The man understood, but he was blocked and that brought a smile to her face. Maybe she could get what she wanted from these fools and entice Amy to the house, for the woman was inexperienced. There was talent, she felt something, but she couldn't channel it. She was an amateur… there was no way she could threaten Matron.

Only Rosie wouldn't keep down. She surged into Matron's mind and shouted in her head. There was hope and excitement in her thoughts and Matron couldn't allow that. So she piled pain and humiliation on Rosie's mind, but the woman kept fighting back. It was as if she was a boxer, trained for endurance and for power.

Matron jerked as she sent more pain, but this time it worked as she felt Rosie withdraw. Before she could celebrate her victory, her fingers touched the brown-haired woman, and a shock greater than any she had ever felt bolted through her.

This woman may be inexperienced but she was dangerous. It was time to go before she suspected anything.

Matron sprang to her feet, hiding her fear as she turned to go.

"Rosie, what is it?" Amy shouted.

Why wouldn't the idiotic woman just do as she was instructed? Well, hopefully Matron had convinced her she was a friend, and she could salvage something from this meeting.

"I really want to see your computer," Gail said, and she bobbed in her seat.

Was she about to stand or actually giving some reverence? It was hard to tell, but Matron wouldn't trust her, not now.

"I changed my mind," Matron said, and wished she could understand why she was here. "Amy come and have a coffee with me, soon. I demand your company."

Fear was like a snake curled in her gut. It was strange to feel something so alien and she didn't like it. As she tried to walk, her legs were weak and her fingers were shaking. This wouldn't do. No, this wouldn't do at all. If she saw these two again then she would kill them and add them to her harem of souls.

Once through the door she felt better, her legs moving faster. She raced down the street and away from the café as fast as she could.

* * *

"Oh my God!" Gail said, as the café door swung closed behind Rosie's retreating body. She had rushed out of there in the strangest of ways. Bent over and then rushing forward. The sneer on her face and the ridiculous demand, that was no doubt meant to sound friendly. The only thing Gail didn't understand was why Jesse wouldn't let her follow.

Surely if they stopped the spirit now then it would be better for Rosie, better for everyone. She sensed something so dark it scared her and that was saying a lot. Gail had seen her share of bad spirits and hauntings. She had been scared, terrified, but this time she felt desolate and small. It was so strange.

Jesse was looking at her and smiling. He nodded to see that she was listening and then he turned to Amy.

"You need to tell us everything," he said, his voice firm,

commanding, and yet there was something in the tone that made her want to trust him.

Amy was fighting back her tears. Her hands were on top of the table clasping and unclasping in a kind of compulsive fashion. She looked close to going into shock.

"Amy," Jesse lowered his voice even further. "We can help her, but we have to know everything."

Amy let the tears fall and sobbed openly. The few patrons in the café looked for a moment, but then had the good manners to turn back to their meals. To leave them in peace.

Gail got up from her chair and went to sit next to Amy. She handed her a handkerchief and put a gentle hand on her shoulder.

The tears slowed. Amy looked up, wiped her eyes, blew her nose and then gulped hard. She was fighting for control and it looked like she was winning.

"I wanted to tell someone, but I'm so afraid of getting Rosie into trouble. She could go to jail for what has been done and I truly don't think it's her fault."

"You really do need to tell us everything," Gail said as she rubbed her shoulder.

Amy sniffed and nodded. "I know. I told you how strange Rosie's been. You've now seen that. It's as if she's fighting a battle for her body." Amy stopped and looked at Gail. Her eyes were wide and unbelieving. She was challenging Gail to laugh at her.

Gail nodded. "She is. We understand and I can feel the spirit, I can see her beneath the façade of Rosie's face. I can also see your friend. She's strong and she's fighting. She won't give in, but we need to know everything to help her."

Amy's mouth relaxed and her shoulders sank. "I thought I was going crazy... I heard Amy talking about... about... she was arguing with herself. Then I saw a bloody handprint on her wall. It was just after... oh it is so awful, I can't tell you. If I'm wrong I could destroy her life."

Jesse took Amy's hand. "You will destroy her life if you let this spirit take over. She is strong and she is ancient. I believe she is what is known as an Old Hag. They possess people by taking souls. They force those souls to submit to their will and then those poor people become the spirits power base. Usually... usually though, they are stuck in a property."

"Then how did she get here?"

Jesse looked at Gail he didn't like what he had to say. He almost couldn't' believe it himself, but it was the only explanation. For a moment, he wanted to leave the café and take some time. To contact his Spirit Guides and ask them for help. But that was stupid and pointless. It had been weeks since any of them would make contact with him.

Gail smiled. She trusted him, and for a second he closed his eyes and concentrated. Drawing on all his experience, he centered his mind and asked himself the question. *Has an Old Hag possessed Rosie?*

Taking a deep breath he waited for his mind to clear and the answer to come. Instead, he heard a voice.

"Yes."

CHAPTER 21

Jesse couldn't believe that his grandmother, Sylvia, was finally communicating with him. She was the most elusive of his Spirit Guides and had spoken to him only once many years ago. For months he had been trying to contact his Spirit Guides and had achieved nothing, zero, squat, nada.

His childhood dog Rose, the big brindle boxer that was such a big part of his youth, had helped him out on a few occasions. She had saved Gail's life and led them where they needed to go.

Occasionally she would touch his mind and appear before him bringing a feeling of love and warmth.

Then there was the old man, laughing and strange, he had appeared to Jesse since he was a child. Once he had helped, but it was hard to know what his motivations were. In the past, his presence was disturbing more than helpful.

It frustrated him that the person he always wanted to contact, his grandmother, Sylvia. The one who knew so much about spirits and how to deal with them had resolutely refused to be contacted, even when Jesse was in dire need of help. *Why?*

Because you don't need me, Sylvia whispered inside his mind.

"I do," he spoke the words aloud and ignored the strange looks from Amy and Gail. "I often need your support and counsel."

No, you don't; you just think you do. Jesse, my beautiful boy you are so talented, and yet you block that talent through fear and guilt. Neither are justified nor necessary. Let them go and you can help so many.

Jesse felt his world turning and his mind struggled to keep up. He knew why he had the guilt. He had caused his grandfather, Sylvia's husband, to die. That was fact, and even though he was just a boy, he should have known better.

"How did she get here?" Amy asked again.

Jesse raised his hand to stop her speaking, but he knew she was right. He had to bring his mind back to the job at hand. How could he save Rosie from this possession?

"She has possessed this girl, taken control of her body, and is using it to... to move about, but why?" Jesse was talking to both Amy and Sylvia.

Trust your instincts and reach for your power. Sylvia's voice was fading. *You know what is happening and you must be strong if you are to save this woman's soul. Amy has the answers you seek. You must push her to get them. Be strong, my boy. This one is tricky, mean, and dangerous. You must not fear or you will all die.*

For a moment, he could smell a sweet lavender perfume and he was wrapped in warm loving arms. It took him back to his childhood and filled him with both joy and sadness. There was so much he wanted to ask. So much he wanted to say. Bathing in the feeling, he ordered his thoughts. He was determined to tell her he was sorry for Charles, for his grandfather, but before he could speak, the warmth was gone and he knew that Sylvia was gone, also. She would not answer him again. All he could do was take her advice and help – if he could.

"I'm sorry, Amy. I was just talking to one of my Spirit Guides. Just confirming what I already know. There is a spirit called Old Hag. She is ancient and malevolent. Normally she takes souls, binds them to her and forces them to work for her. But she has not only stolen Rosie's soul, she has stolen her body. It is unheard of, unprecedented, and we must be careful in how we deal with her. I need to know everything if we are to help her, for if we don't help soon, it will be too late."

Amy's eyes widened. The fear was apparent in her pale, waxy complexion, in the way her hands circled each other, and the nerve that jumped in her jaw. Her mouth opened; her moist eyes spoke volumes but the words wouldn't come. She lowered her eyes to the table and picked up her coffee mug. Taking a large swallow of what must now be cold, she gulped and almost spluttered.

"You can talk to us." Jesse reached out and took the cup from her hand. "I understand, some of this must be hard and difficult, but you can talk to us."

Amy's eyes rose. Tears brimmed beneath her lashes, holding on by sheer force of will alone. "You don't understand. I can't betray her. I can't do this — what friend could?"

Gail took Amy's hands in hers." Trust us."

Amy looked at Gail. It was the look of a drowning woman

who can see the shoreline but is not quite sure that she can swim that far. There was desperation, hope, fear, and resignation in that look. The knowledge that she had to swim as fast and as far as she could. That she had to give it all, if there was any chance of survival. Dropping her head, she nodded.

"I heard Rosie speaking about killing someone," Amy said, taking her eyes off the table. "It was as if she was talking to someone, arguing with someone, and yet the voice that answered back was hers and not hers. How does that even make sense?"

"What did she say exactly?" Jesse asked.

Amy was quiet for so long that he thought that she would not answer. Then she took in a deep breath. "I can't remember the exact words but she was arguing about who had been killed. Then she replied in a voice so cold it stopped me dead. She said that she would kill all of her friends, including me."

"Did you ever ask her about this?" Jesse knew he had to keep pushing, but maybe there was a simple explanation and that had to be ruled out first. That was the number one decree when dealing with the paranormal... always rule out the normal before you believe in the paranormal.

Amy looked up and there was hope in her eyes. "I did. She said she was running through a scene from her book... The problem is I've read her books and there has never been a murder, not even the hint of violence in any of them. There was something about the way she spoke to me. At times I thought she was talking in code, that she was hiding things from somebody else. Other times she was arrogant and cruel. Nothing like the person I know. I just don't understand any of this." She pulled her hand free from Gail's and dropped them hard onto the table. The thump caused a few heads to turn.

Jesse knew she was holding back. That there was something worse, but he needed to gain her trust before he pushed any harder.

"I believe your friend is very clever and very strong. She has worked out that this spirit does not understand the modern world. When Rosie is speaking, there is confidence. When the Old Hag talked about the computer, it is obvious she has no idea what it is. The way she demanded you come to see her, and yet she was trying to be your friend. This shows she does not understand relationships. Rosie has given us hints and shown us that she is still there. I am hoping she is strong enough to help, but I need to know everything. I know this is hard but you can't hold back."

Amy wiped the tears that had started to trace down her face, and she nodded.

"I visited Rosie the night after the first murder. That was when I heard her talking about killing. When she let me in there was a bloody handprint on the staircase, and it seemed as if she was fighting with herself. I have tried to find a rational explanation. Maybe she cut herself?"

"Do you really believe that?"

"No."

Jesse could see the pain that this was causing Amy and he kept quiet, giving her time to come to terms with what she must say.

Beneath the table, he gently touched Gail's leg with his own. She had seemed to understand the situation and was learning how he worked, but this was a critical point. They had to let Amy come to terms with this and tell them in her own time.

Gail reached out and took his hand beneath the table, squeezing it and giving him the support he needed. They could do this. They could help this girl. Though her life would never be the same. Jesse feared she had some terrible things to face. Things she didn't deserve, but still she would be alive and her soul would be intact.

"There is more I have to tell you," Amy said, her voice little more than a whisper. "Rosie lived with an abusive boyfriend. No doubt you saw her scars. That was why I persuaded her to visit RedRise House to house sit. I thought she would be safe there, that it would give her time to heal." Amy held back her tears and carried on. "She was never the same after that but... I bought her a present. It was a necklace I had seen her looking at."

Jesse felt his stomach flip as he knew what was coming.

"It was a crystal rose on a silver chain. It was found on the second victim's body." Amy's voice choked and she broke down into tears.

Gail got up and went around the table. She slid into the chair next to Amy and pulled her into her arms. Hugging her close, she rubbed her back and just let her cry.

At last Amy sat up and looked across at Jesse. "She killed those people, didn't she?"

Jesse nodded. "Most likely."

More tears slid from Amy's eyes as she understood her choice. Stop a killer and send her friend to jail.

CHAPTER 22

Matron raced down the street as if the devil was on her heels. Fear pushed her in a way she had never felt before. The young body rushed forward, strong, athletic and yet she stumbled more than she should have. It was like she was running out of control down a hill so steep that any moment she would fall, tumble, and plummet to her death.

No! She could not die, could not fail. Now that she had finally escaped RedRise House she had to survive, to grow, to conquer.

Arriving back at Rosie's, she fumbled for the key and then remembered she hadn't bothered to lock the door. Why would she? None of the material things mattered to her. Besides, if anyone tried to come in, her acolytes would drive them out.

That brought a smile to her face and calmed her nerves. She had power. Not the power she had before. Not the dozens of young lives that she had left behind in RedRise. Young sacrifices gave so much power. Their life force was vital, strong, and encompassing. So far, she had only taken one youthful life… the drunken boy she now knew was called James.

He still didn't understand what had happened. He thought that he was still drunk. It amused her to watch him try and leave the house. He would get about 50 yards from the door and then bounce back with a bemused look on his face. It was fun, but she needed him to submit to give her his full power.

He was fighting her still, unlike the first two who had accepted their fate.

Geoffrey had even welcomed it and would become her most trusted acolyte in time. He believed that he had been saved, transformed, and he savored the darkness.

Mary was not so pliable and was stronger than she looked. The fool sympathized with Rosie, but that would come to nothing. Rosie was fading and soon she would be naught but a memory.

Matron locked the door and walked up the stairs. Passing the bedroom and the table with the horrible fake flowers, she walked to the room that Rosie hated. It was the one she had shared with Clive. Matron hadn't been able to get all the details about her relationship, but she knew that Rosie was scared of the man.

In this room she had made an altar. It wasn't much, but it bound her spirits, her souls to this house and it gave her power.

A small table was covered with her black altar cloth and on the wall behind it was a pentagram. Drawn in Mary's blood. It dripped occasionally as though it were a living thing.

On the table were two candle sticks in black, and her book. It was open to a blank page. Sitting down she picked up a pen, wanting to record the day's events, but she hesitated, dropping the pen. What had happened today was the closest she had come to failure and she would not record it. She would never fail.

Closing her eyes, she pushed back fear and despair. These were things she should inflict, not suffer. Rosie, that foolish girl, was the cause of all her problems. She had to break her will.

It had been harder than she expected keeping Rosie from taking control. Fatigue weighed heavy on her shoulders, like wet furs that dragged her down. To control Rosie, she needed more… more lives, more souls, and one of them had to be Amy's. Would she come?

Matron delved into her mind searching for Rosie's thoughts. The fool thought that she was hiding from her, but she didn't understand. Matron knew all, felt all, and understood all.

So she pushed and shoved against the barrier in her mind, searching for the weak link that would snap and let her in. All she wanted was to find out if Amy would come.

Silence filled her mind… silence and nothing. Whatever Rosie was doing was keeping her out and it drove Matron wild.

Tell me!" she screamed in Rosie's mind. *Tell me when she will come*

Nothing.

THE BATTLE WITHIN

Matron launched herself from the room and ran down the stairs to the insipid kitchen. Rage filled her and she looked for someone to hurt. There was no one about, no one outside on the streets. Fury filled her and she swept everything off the counter.

A cacophony of crashes and bangs echoed off the dull beige walls and rattled against the blood-red blind as canisters of coffee, tea, and sugar hit the tiled floor. The more they crashed, the more intense her fury, and they were followed by mugs, a teapot, and a potted spider plant.

Wrath controlled Matron as she tore pictures from the walls and threw them to the floor. Opening a cupboard, she swept all the cups from the shelves. Seeing them fly through the air filled her with satisfaction, but as they crashed to the floor her, legs gave way and she crumpled down and landed amid the debris.

Weakness sucked her down like quicksand would capture an unwary animal. At first she struggled, afraid of the way it pulled her toward oblivion as it lulled, soothed, and pacified. Soon she welcomed, not having to think or to fight the noise and bustle of this new world, and she succumbed to the darkness that was nothing. Just for a little while, she would rest.

Rosie felt Matron let go and took full control of her body for the first time in a long while. Her hunger was no longer painful. It had been hard ignoring her need to eat, and difficult hiding the meaning of the pain, but it was worth it. Matron was exhausted, malnourished, and weak.

Now all she had to decide was how she could take advantage of the situation.

As if in answer, a dark shadow crossed the room and stopped

just in front of her. Slowly it formed into the shape of an old lady. Out of the darkness she could see the hint of pink and a smile.

* * *

"Can we stop her killing?" Amy asked.

Jesse understood the unasked question. Could they save Rosie… could they rid her of the possession, or would they have to kill them both? It was a question he was not ready to answer, but even a slight hesitation here might cause them the loss of Amy's help, and so he lied. "Yes, we will be able to exorcise the Old Hag from your friend. Rosie will be fine."

A greasy coil of guilt turned in his stomach like a snake settling down for the duration. It made him want to quit. To run from here and to give in.

Trust your instincts and reach for your power.

He remembered the words Sylvia had spoken not ten minutes ago. Gail was his power; was that what Sylvia meant? It didn't feel right. Did she mean that he still had his talent? That he could become sensitive again?

It was what he had wanted since that day. Since the meeting with the Black-Eyed Children, the death of his grandfather, and the loss of his talent. All his life since then he had been searching to regain his abilities, and now Sylvia had hinted that he may be blocking himself. No, it couldn't be true. But even if it was, he had to help Rosie and there was no time to rediscover his abilities. Speed was of the essence if they were to prevent the Old Hag from taking more lives — but the question was how?

Trust your instincts and reach for your power.

It sounded so simple and yet he knew it would be anything but. For now he would trust his instincts and he would be careful.

"We need to go and see Rosie," he said, "but we have to prepare first. Can you give us the address and please make sure you don't go to see her? She may try and cajole you into visiting, but it is of the utmost importance that you don't. At the moment, she wants you dead. Needs you dead. Do you understand?"

Amy shook her head, and the color drained from her face. "I have to be there; I can help."

Jesse was about to say no when Gail touched his leg.

"You can come, but it will be hard, harrowing, and possibly dangerous," Gail said. "If you understand all that, and do exactly as we say, then we will take you with us."

Jesse bit down on the retort that was perched on the edge of his tongue. Having Amy there would make things much worse and it would be extremely dangerous. There was a possibility that Old Hag would jump from one person to the next. Hopefully, he and Gail would be safe. They wore protection, but it was wrong for Gail to suggest this. Maybe he needed to talk to her and tell her not to speak unless she checked with him first.

As he had that thought he felt heat hit his cheeks. If he had said that aloud she would smack him around the head, a proper Gibbs slap, and he would deserve it.

Amy was nodding. "I will do what you ask."

"That means leaving if we ask, too," Gail said.

Amy nodded.

Jesse bit back his anger and they all left the café. "We will meet back here in one hour," he said. "If we are late, wait; do not go see her alone."

Amy nodded.

Soon Jesse climbed into the jeep and turned the car away from the town. He wasn't going home. All he needed was the time to talk to Gail and to prepare them both. His car was packed with everything they needed and lots they didn't. Cold spot meters, infra-red cameras, EMF meters were all redundant. They knew a spirit was there and all they had to do was exorcise it.

All!

Jesse found a quiet road and pulled over. He was still angry and still wanted to stop Amy coming with them, but he didn't know how to broach the subject.

A hand reached out and touched his shoulder. Looking at Gail, he could see that she knew she had upset him.

Her brown eyes were defiant and yet worried, and his heart melted. He couldn't be angry with her, but he had to explain the danger she had put Amy in.

Before he could talk she cut him off with a raised hand.

"I know you don't want Amy to come, but she wasn't going to give us the address unless we invited her."

"I could have gotten it out of her," Jesse snapped.

"You're right, you probably could have... but could you get the Old Hag to open the door for us?"

CHAPTER 23

Amy sat in the back of the Jeep, deathly quiet and ghostly pale.

Jesse caught a glance of her in the rearview mirror. Had it been the right decision to bring her? Seeing her here, her hair so fashionable and chic. So confident, and yet now she bit her lip and fear widened her eyes. Knowing they were taking her into danger curdled his stomach and made his jaw ache. But now he had had a chance to think about it, he understood Gail's logic. They needed the Old Hag to let them in and the spirit wanted Amy.

Gail sat in the passenger seat. Her hand constantly went to her neck and the turquoise necklace hanging there. Just two days ago he had dipped that necklace and the black bracelet he wore in holy water while blessing them both. It cleansed them, giving them protective properties, and helped prevent the wearer from being possessed. Maybe they should have gotten something similar for Amy.

It was all he could do to not turn around as he remembered a time when Gail had been possessed. Her talent was so strong that he thought she would never succumb, and he had made the mistake of leaving her vulnerable. Was he making the same mistake here?

There was so much to think about. Amy had insisted on coming, Gail had agreed. He was the one with no power and he had to go along with the decision. All he had was experience and knowledge — would that be enough?

The acid in his stomach told him everything he needed to know. They were in trouble.

They had to force the spirit out of Rosie and it may try to control Amy. Why had he allowed her to come? Maybe they could leave her outside. Maybe he could help protect her with what they had in the car. The thoughts circled his brain like a never-ending carousel. Round and round until they all blended into one.

"Jesse!" Gail called. "We're here."

Jesse knew that if he didn't take control, then Gail would. She was strong, full of natural talent, and excited about the spirit world. It was still new to her and she had beaten everything she had faced. Exuding confidence, she was ready for battle, but would it be enough?

"Good." He jumped from the Jeep and went to the back. Opening up the door, he looked inside. All the equipment was at the back. They wouldn't need that.

"We don't need meters," Gail said. "We should just go in. I feel that time is running short."

Jesse put his hand on her arm. "We go in, but we do this my way. We go in prepared and we stay safe."

THE BATTLE WITHIN

"Does Rosie have time for this?" Amy's eyes were wide and defiant, but tears had dried on her cheeks.

"We can't help her if we're dead." Jesse turned from the women and searched through the compartments he had filled over the years. In the bottom somewhere were some velvet bags and some copper wiring. He found them and then searched for a crystal and some white sage. It didn't take long. Everything was neatly sorted and stored. The order gave him confidence.

Piling the bits he had found into the velvet bag, he grabbed three bottles of holy water and splashed some onto the drawstring bag. Handing one bottle to both women he stowed the third in his pocket. Holding the bag in his left hand he closed his.

"Hurry," Amy said, and started toward the house.

Without opening his eyes Jesse, reached out and grabbed her arm. He pulled her back. "We will do this right."

Feeling her relax, he let go and breathed deeply. Going inside he trusted his instincts and waited. The urge to call on his spirit guides was strong even though he knew they wouldn't appear. "Oh guides who protect me, lend me your energies and give me your power to conquer the evil we are about to face."

The feeling of strength and healing light filled him, and so did confidence. Maybe he did have something to offer here.

"Bless and cleanse this totem and keep safe all who wear it. Guide them to find the truth and the place of light. Guide me to send this spirit back to the darkness and to keep Rosie safe."

At the mention of that name, so similar to that of his most

loving spirit guide, his dog, he felt Rose join him. She sat before him, her tongue hanging out of her big black face. Many people would say dogs can't smile, but she was surely happy to be there, and he was instantly enveloped in her love.

"Keep us safe as we enter the darkness and guide us to the light." Shaking his head he sent her his love.

Opening his eyes he could see the women looking at him. They were staring and he knew that his confidence was high. Something had changed, and although none of them knew what it was, they could all feel it.

Taking the totem bag, he tied it to a string and gave it to Amy. For a moment it looked as if she would disagree. His hand hung between them, the little bag swinging. Jesse wouldn't pull back. She either wore it or she stayed out, and maybe she saw his resolve, as she accepted the bag and tied it around her neck.

"Okay, let's do this," he said.

Amy approached the door first and knocked. "Hey Rosie, I'm here."

They waited. The house was dark, too dark, and standing beneath its shadow filled them with a feeling of foreboding.

Ignoring the chill, Jesse reached out and tried the handle. It was sealed; they were not getting in without the Old Hag's help.

Amy knocked again. "Rosie, you wanted to see me… well, I'm here."

* * *

Rosie could hear her friend at the door. With all her heart she wanted to let her in, but she knew she couldn't. Matron had made it clear that she wanted Amy dead and she knew that she didn't have the power to stop her. Hunger, fatigue, and the constant pain had all taken its toll. Even at her strongest, she doubted she could fight the spirit, but now she had little chance – no chance, if she was honest. Mary had helped her, offered her hope, and given her a way out. She trusted she would have the strength to carry it through. But, if Amy got in and Matron took more souls, then all would be lost.

Ignoring her friends, she went upstairs to make the final arrangements. Quickly throwing a few items into her a bag, including Clive's cut-throat razor, she searched for her phone.

At last she found it, and was pleased that the battery still had some power... enough to send a text.

> *Amy, I love you, but I have a plan.*
> *I can't explain, but I have to do this alone.*
> *Please leave.*
> *Thank you for always being there.*
> *Rosie xxx*

Once that was done, she sat down in the corner of the room and waited. The knocking on the door stopped and she let out a sigh. Amy would do as she asked. Soon this would be over and her friend would be safe.

* * *

"Rosie, come on, we need to talk," Amy said, as she knocked

on the door again. A buzz from her phone stopped her and she pulled it from her pocket. "Oh!"

"What?" Gail asked.

Amy showed them both the text. "We can't leave her, can we?" Amy's eyes were so big in her white face that she looked like an Anime doll.

"No, we can't leave, but you can," Jesse said. "Your friend is fighting and it's clear she won't let you in. If we act quickly before the spirit regains control, then we have a chance."

"I won't leave." Amy folded her arms and blocked the way. "I can help you. I can get through to her."

Jesse wanted to pull her from the door. Didn't she understand when the spirit was in control, there was no Rosie? All they could do was try and force it out, but the more he thought about, it the more he knew they wouldn't be able to do so. All they could do was end it and make sure there was nowhere for the spirit to escape to. That way she would die with Rosie.

Amy's eyes opened wide and her jaw dropped. She had seen through his intentions.

CHAPTER 24

"No!" Amy shouted, and she rushed forward, beating at Jesse with her bunched fists. He reacted quickly and raised his arms to protect his face, but all he could do was defend. She was right to be angry, right to hate him for what he knew he had to do.

"I have no choice," he said.

"Stop it!" Gail shouted, and she pulled Amy away, putting herself between the two of them. "What is going on?"

"He's going to kill her," Amy stuttered between sobs.

"No, don't be silly, he's..." Gail's voice broke as she turned to Jesse and it broke his heart to see the look on her face. All these years she hadn't believed in the supernatural, but she had believed in him. Seeing that look on her face was enough to weaken his knees, but what choice did he have? "No you wouldn't?" Gail said, but the break in her voice was clear.

"I have no choice." Jesse reached out to take her hands, but she pulled away.

"There is always a choice and I won't be part of this."

"Gail, listen to me. How many people would you see die? Me, you, Amy? If we go in there with less than full resolve, then this spirit will cut through us like a hot knife through butter. Then she'll be loose in the world and her reign could last forever, taking more and more lives to exist. We have a chance to stop her. If I can, I will save Rosie, but if not, then we have to end this and we have to do it now."

Gail's mouth opened. Her eyes blazed but she couldn't form the words. "I... I..."

Jesse looked down at the ground and then back at the two women. "I will do my very best to save Rosie. I promise, but we have to be clear. This spirit, the Old Hag, has to die. Many more lives are at stake and we have to make that choice now. Gail, with your help we have a chance to save her… without it…"

"I hate this," Amy said. "But I understand what you are saying. As long as you promise to try, I am with you."

Jesse nodded. "I promise I will try. Gail?"

Gail nodded, but she couldn't look at him, and that hurt almost as much as what they had to face.

"There is a key around the back." Amy pointed. "Follow me."

Jesse grabbed Gail's arm and she spun around to face him. Her eyes were bright with unshed tears and her lip quivered, but the set of her jaw showed resolve and anger.

"I'm sorry," he said, "but we have to be strong. I would give anything to not do this, to not say those words, but sometimes there is no choice."

Gail nodded and gave him a faint smile. "Make a choice," she said, and followed Amy.

Even with the key, Jesse knew they wouldn't be able to get in. The Old Hag was strong and ancient and if she wanted them kept out, then the door would be sealed.

Amy pulled the key from a faded frog that was hidden in the garden. With a sad smile she handed it over.

Jesse took it and pulled back at the cold and slightly damp metal. Ignoring the feeling it gave him, he slid it into the lock and turned. The tumblers moved and he took a breath as he reached for the handle. Would they get in?

The handle turned and he pulled the door. *Nothing!* It didn't even give. The spirit no doubt sealed the house without even thinking as she entered. She had taken three lives that they knew of. There may be more. It was surprising how many people could go missing without anyone ever reporting them, how they could be lost or murdered and no one would ever notice. If only three, they might have a chance, but if she had taken more, then the battle was already lost.

"Why aren't you going in?" Amy asked, her hands on her hips.

"The door is sealed."

"Sealed!" She rushed forward and pulled on the handle. The door didn't budge. Still, she pulled, pushed, and then kicked at the faded wood. "Oooh!" The sound was filled with anger, frustration, despair, and fear. It summed up exactly what Jesse was feeling.

"Maybe I can connect with her," Gail said, and reached forward to put her hand on the window.

Jesse stopped her. "No, not this spirit, not this time." The darkness he had felt and seen was too much. If Gail did this, she would make contact, and it could be the last thing she ever did.

He pulled his Holy Water from his pocket and crossed himself as he approached the door. "Lord Almighty, allow us passage. Let Your light shine on this place. Let Your love fill it and guide those inside back to the path." He threw the Holy Water onto the lock. It sizzled and hissed.

Jesse tried again, but the door still wouldn't budge. It looked like he would have to try all the tricks he knew to even get into the place. Would he have anything left with which to fight?

* * *

INSIDE, Rosie sat in the corner and waited for her friend to leave. Everything was planned. There was a remote Island that Mary had told her about. If she went there and used the razor, then Matron would be trapped. All she had to do was keep in control for long enough to make the journey and to then take that razor and pull it across her own throat.

Could she do it?

The sound of knocking jerked her back to the present. They had to go. With every knock she could feel Matron waking. There was no way she could drive to Scotland. But maybe she could make it back to RedRise House.

If she got there then all she had to do was kill herself, then Matron would be trapped the same as she was before. If she could manage to free a few of the children first, then all the better. It would reduce the spirit's power and help the children. Now as she thought about it, this was a much better plan and she felt hope, real hope for the first time in a long while.

Knock, knock. "Rosie, I thought you wanted to talk."

She tried to shut out the voice and to push Matron away, but the evil inside her was waking. Like insects in her mind, it buzzed and surged. Soon the noise would be unbearable and she would lose control. She didn't have long. "Leave me alone, Amy. Please leave."

CHAPTER 25

Inside Matron's head the girl fought, plotted, and pushed her down. It was insufferable, intolerable, and she would not allow it. Apparently, Rosie was stronger than she'd imagined, and the possession had been tougher than she expected. She was still weak… too weak.

If she could call on her acolytes it would help, but Rosie stopped her at every try. How could this happen? She had planned this escape for so long. Had picked a person weak and beaten. One who shouldn't have fought back—but she did. *Stop this! Give in!"* she screamed in her mind.

"Never," Rosie answered without hesitation, and her voice was strong. Too strong.

Matron needed to get to her altar, or to at least hold onto her necklace. But, she sat here in this corner. The floor hurt her back, and her arms and legs refused to budge. She was trapped in another prison. One worse than RedRise House. One of her own making and one she was determined to escape.

If she could just get up and go to the spare room. It was a room Rosie hated. It had once been the room she shared with a man named Clive. Matron had known some of her story before selecting Rosie. It had been difficult, but she had worked out more since the possession.

Rosie had loved the man who beat her. The one who left her scarred and burned and broken. It had taken her a long while to let go, and she lived with that guilt. To Matron it was pathetic. What fool would let a man hurt them? What fool would weaken themselves for love?

That was one of the reasons she had chosen that specific room for her altar. It would weaken Rosie each time she was in it.

She had set up her seat of power there. It was just a simple table with a cloth, her book, and a pentagram drawn in blood. Once it was blessed with a dark incantation, it gave her power and an anchor for her acolytes. There, the spirits she took would have to obey her. There, she could go when the world felt too foreign, too bright, too shiny, or too good.

Or she could simply hold the necklace that hung around her neck. It felt heavy and cold, and was so close, but these foolish arms refused to move.

Once more she gritted her metaphoric teeth and tried to reach for the necklace. The body she occupied stayed as still as a comatose patient on death watch. Frustration boiled inside her and as she could feel the arms moving and yet they resolutely refused to budge. A scream echoed around her mind, but Rosie didn't even flinch.

The girl was strong, but Matron was eternal. She had time, she could wait, and one day she would kill Amy, then, Rosie's mind would break. So she imagined getting to her altar and grasping the necklace.

Either of these would help her to call on her acolytes, but even they seemed to be working against her. Except for Geoffrey. Thinking about him filled her with delight. He was dark, evil, cold, and he would help her. *No, my beauty, you wait a little longer,* she whispered to him as he started to materialize.

If Rosie was going to fight, then Matron had to be clever. Relaxing, she let her exhaustion wash over her. This human body was so weak and frail. Often there was a pain in her stomach and she would stumble and almost fall. It had been so long since she was human that these weaknesses vexed her. But, she could use that to her advantage. Feigning a weakness that was worse than she felt, she pulled back into the deep recesses of Rosie's mind. There she hid in the dark, waiting, watching, and building her strength. She was evil, eternal, and stronger than this weak and pathetic human — she would prevail. All she needed to do was to wait for an opportunity.

Rosie relaxed as Matron pulled back. "Amy, please leave. I have a plan but you have to leave or she will kill you."

The pounding on the door stopped.

"Rosie, let us in. These people can help you. We know what is happening. We know about the Old Hag and the possession. Let us in... let us help."

Jesse sprinkled Holy water on the lock of the door and placed his hand on the wood. "Keep talking... the seal is weakening."

Rosie leaned back against the cold wall and tried to shut out her friend's voice. But what if Amy was right? What if they could help? Fatigue weighed her down and the thought of fighting Matron was more than she could bear. Maybe she should let them in, give in, and let them take over.

The more she thought about it the more she believed it was the right thing to do. She started to stand. Matron was afraid of the two people, Jesse and Gail. She felt their power and believed they could hurt her. So this had to be the right thing to do.

Only Rosie knew that Matron was clever. Maybe she was using her, letting her feel this to allow Amy in. Rosie knew that it *would* break her mind if she killed Amy. She wouldn't be able to live with herself. No matter what happened to her, if she died, if she stayed under the control of this beast forever, it didn't matter, as long as she saved Amy.

Getting to her feet, she searched her mind... pushing and pulling, searching and shining a light in all the dark places. Matron hid amongst her base emotions. Fear, greed, jealousy. They were places she didn't like to look into, places she wanted to avoid, but she searched through them. Feeling the bile and angst hidden there, Matron was nowhere to be found. Surely it was safe.

She took a step toward the door. With each step, she stopped and looked inside. Tasting the air to see if Matron was waiting. Finding her mind blank, empty, she took another step and hope surged inside once more. The brightness of it filled her mind and chased away the darkness. Maybe this was how she would beat the spirit.

If she was to stay strong and be filled with the purity of hope, surely it was too much for such evil to bear.

With each step she grew more confident, more positive that she was alone, that she was herself again.

Little did she know that Matron was waiting, planning, and that she rejoiced in the dark.

"Rosie, are you there? I love you so much and I want to help you!" Amy shouted through the door.

"I'm here." Tears fell from Amy's eyes as she heard the love in her friend's voice. How could she have ever doubted that Amy would save her? Her friend could cope with anything. No matter what life threw at her, she just took it in her stride and always with a smile on her face.

Rosie took three steps and stopped to check inside. Did she feel a stirring, a greasy sickness that spread cold through the back of her mind?

She searched for Matron. "Where are you?" she screamed, but there was no answer… just darkness, shadows, and cold.

"Can you open the door?" Amy called.

"I'm close, just let me take my time." Rosie had to be sure that it was her will that was doing this and she would take as long as it took.

A shadow crossed the room in front of her with a darkness that coalesced and swarmed. It loomed just beyond the corner of her eye. Each time she tried to look, to focus, it was gone, and yet she knew that it wanted her to see.

"Mary?"

The shadow formed in front of her and from out of the mist, a face appeared, contorted into a scream. But then, it was gone as quickly as it appeared.

"Mary, I'm so sorry." Tears formed in Rosie's eyes. She had killed this woman. This kind and good person's blood had run down her hands as she plunged a knife into her throat. Stepping forward, she was now just a few paces from the door. "Mary, can I help you?"

The shadow was back, between her and the door. At first it was just a mist, just a feeling of dark, fleeting, ephemeral, and transitory. Then it formed, and the hint of pink appeared. This time the spirit had a smile on her face. It lit up her features and made you want to hug her.

The cold was gone and replaced with a feeling of warmth, but Mary was blocking her way. She raised her arms and pointed behind Rosie.

Rosie quickly spun around, but nothing was there.

"What do you want?" she asked, and stepped closer to Mary.

The ghost shook her head, she was fading, drifting away. The anguish on her features was now clear and she shook her head again and pointed. Waving her arms frantically, she made pushing motions at Rosie, and then she was gone.

The room was instantly warmer, but to Rosie it appeared darker and less welcoming. What had Mary wanted? To keep her from the door? That had to be it. Did it mean that Mary knew something? Did she know that Matron was tricking her? Was the evil waiting and wanting her to let Amy in?

It made no sense. Mary was under the control of the spirit. She had been sent to keep her from the door. Maybe the ghost was like an alarm system that Matron had left to keep her safe. That made more sense. Rosie rushed the last few steps to the door and grasped onto the handle.

It never occurred to her that when the ghost was under

Matron's control she was wearing a black cloak and not the pretty pink coat she had died in.

CHAPTER 26

*J*esse concentrated on the door, using every trick, every prayer he could to break the spirit's hold. But he was failing. What they were dealing with was older and more powerful than anything they had ever met… anything he had ever imagined.

Out of the corner of his eye he could see Gail pacing. She wanted to try and contact the spirit. The innate goodness in her believed that she could solve this with words, with negotiation. As much as he wanted to get into the house, to save Rosie, more than anything he wanted to keep Gail safe. Of course, Gail was never one to be cautious. She would rush in wanting to help, not caring if she got hurt in the process.

* * *

Rosie's hand touched the door and a jolt went through her. Like static raging up her arm, it shocked and fizzled. She wanted to pull back, but her arm wouldn't move. Something held it there and turned the handle.

Matron was back. It had all been a ploy. The spirit had let her think that she was in control, and here she was letting her friend in. Maybe to her death… she had done exactly what Matron wanted. A wail of grief sounded in her mind, but her lips didn't move. The door cracked open.

What had she done?

* * *

WHILE HE WAS CONCENTRATING on Gail, Jesse felt the door handle turn and the door pulled away from him.

"You did it!" Gail rushed forward and through the open door. "Rosie, is that you?"

The brown-haired girl nodded, but there was something manic about her eyes, and the scar on her left cheek stood out more than the last time they had met. It seemed new and shiny, like a beacon.

Jesse understood this was just his tired mind making the connection, but he didn't believe that Rosie was the one driving, not for one moment. They had to be so careful.

"Gail wait," he called out, but she had already rushed past him, and before he could move, Amy followed.

She pulled her friend into a hug and Jesse was spared the empty, dead fish eyes of the scarred woman for a moment.

While they hugged, Rosie edged herself around, forcing Jesse and Gail back toward the door. Step by delicate step she pushed them closer without Gail realizing, but Jesse knew what was happening. The spirit was in control and she wanted them outside. Maybe she even feared them. *That was something.*

THE BATTLE WITHIN

Jesse moved to the right to step around Rosie, and as he did, she pulled back from Amy and shrieked. She pushed Amy so hard that the young woman fell against the wall. Then, Rosie launched, not at Jesse, but at Gail.

A knife appeared in her hand. It was big, and evil and the sight of it turned his bowels to ice. For a millisecond, he couldn't move and he watched as Rosie, her face contorted into a malicious grin, dived at his sweet Gail.

Gail froze. The smile dropped from her face, but at the last moment her arm swung out and contacted with Rosie's shoulder. The blow deflected the knife away from her and pushed Rosie back.

Jesse kicked. Pure instinct took over and he reverted to some Tai-Kwan-Do lessons from his youth. His foot impacted with Rosie's wrist, sending the knife spiraling into the air, landing on the floor near Amy with a dull clang.

Still the spirit hardly stopped, flying toward Gail. As Gail moved, she was surrounded by darkness, and he could briefly see the spirit that was in control. She was old, wizened, and evil in appearance. Darkness draped over the woman as she grabbed hold of Gail. Part of him acknowledged what just happened. Maybe if he trusted enough in himself as his grandmother had suggested, then his gift would return. There was no time to think about this… He had to save his love.

"No!" Jesse screamed, and surged toward them. It was too late.

Rosie grabbed Gail and sank her teeth into his beloved's neck. Blood gushed and splashed his face as his hands connected with Rosie's shoulders.

Grasping on, he could feel how skinny she was. Bones jutted through her skin, but he pulled with all his might. As Rosie started to move with him, he wondered if it was the right thing to do. What if her teeth were clasped around Gail's jugular? What if pulling her away would rip open an artery?

It didn't matter, it was the only play he had so he hauled harder. As he felt her start to move, he twisted and then threw Rosie to the other side of the room. She was so light that it was easy, in his adrenaline-fueled state, to launch her through the air.

Gail wavered and dropped to her knees.

Jesse's instinct was to grab her and pull her from the house... to slam the door and run, never to return. But he couldn't. He had to stop the bleeding. He had to help Amy and Rosie... now! "I'm all right," Gail said, as she clasped a hand to her neck.

Jesse grabbed her and rushed her through to what he thought was a kitchen. Pulling her hand away, he stared at the wound. It was raw and angry, but the blood was slowing. Teeth marks were etched deep into her skin, looking like a bite from some rabid dog. They had torn away a small chunk of flesh, leaving behind exposed muscle which wept blood. It looked horrible but was mainly superficial. It could have been so much worse.

Letting out a sigh of relief, he kissed her forehead and looked around for something to make a bandage with.

Amy came from behind him and pointed to a cupboard.

Jesse rushed to it. For a second he wondered if she had picked up the knife. He ignored the blank expression on Amy's face. She was in shock, but there was no time to deal with that now. They would sort it once they were out of here… if they got out of here.

In the cupboard he saw a first aid kit. Quickly, he cleaned the wound and applied some anti-bacterial, gauze and a bandage. It would hold for now, or at least he hoped it would.

Where was the Old Hag, Rosie? After the initial attack, he had expected her to push her advantage. Turning, he could see her on the floor. Her hands were waving in front of her face as though she were a puppet controlled by some crazy master who wanted her to hand jive.

"Gail, I want you to leave." Jesse started to guide her the short distance toward the door. He hoped that he could get her out of there before the spirit took control again.

"Why would I leave?" Gail turned toward him, her eyebrows pulled down with confusion.

"You're hurt. This spirit can't be channeled." He wanted to tell her there was nothing she could do. That she would be a liability, but he knew it was the last thing she wanted to hear. "Let me handle this. You need to lie down after that injury." How he hoped that the concern he felt showed through his voice and that she would believe him.

For a second she nodded her head and started toward the door. But as she passed closer to Rosie, she stopped. "I can't leave. I can't let these two women down. You need me. I know you don't believe it. I know you think that you are keeping me safe, but I know you will need me and I won't leave you."

"Gail, please."

"No, I feel it. Things are going to get bad… but we are in this together." She turned to him and took his hands. "We're stronger together."

The door slammed and the temperature dropped, plunging the room into a sub-zero gloom that filled him with a feeling of such despair and despondency that it almost dropped him to his knees. "No." The word left his mouth without him even realizing it and filled his mind with anguish.

Against the wall, Rosie's hands stopped in mid-air. For a moment, they hovered in front of her like two broken birds hoping they could still fly. Behind them, her face morphed and mutated, changing from the sweet scarred girl to the old hag and back again. Sometimes they could see the skull of the spirit through the pink of Rosie's skin and at others, there was a darkness. A shadow was surrounding her and shielding the real person beneath.

As they stared, she rose from the ground like a puppet hauled to its feet. Her arms were still hanging in front of her, and Jesse saw the pendant around her neck. He understood.

It was a pentagram, very old, probably pewter, and it would be part of her power. Rosie was fighting. She was fighting Matron, preventing her from touching it and maybe, if he could rip it from her neck, then he could send this bitch back to the hell hole from where she came.

Filled with new hope, he surged forward, reaching out to grab the necklace.

Rosie's face mirrored his hope and then filled with triumph. Jesse smiled. She understood and believed that he could make it happen. She would help him. Then he saw the malice in that triumphant smile and realized that the spirit was back.

Hand outstretched, he lunged for the necklace — he was so close. The world slowed down as he watched Rosie's arms start to move. She reaching for the necklace at the same time as he was. It was a race, and his life, Gail's life depended on the outcome.

Almost flying now, he stretched just a little more, almost feeling the cold, weighty metal in his fingers.

Rosie stepped back and he crash-landed on the floor at her feet. Looking up, he saw the gleam of victory in her eyes as her hands both clasped onto the necklace. She made a batting motion in the air.

Jesse was picked up and thrown across the room. The air was knocked from his lungs as he hit the wall, and was then sent flying again, only to hit the wall in the living room, sliding down to the floor behind the sofa.

Gasping for breath, he tried to move, but found the air was thick and heavy, like a weight was pressing him into the floor.

Darkness settled over the room and prevented him from seeing Gail. Where was she? Was she safe? He had to get her out of here. Things had gone too far. They were losing the battle. Now all he could focus on was escape. Maybe they could regroup; maybe they should simply burn this house to the ground and salt the ashes, but first they had to escape.

"Gail!" he shouted.

"She's okay." Amy sidled over to him, remaining on the floor.

"And you?"

"I'm good, but I think Rosie has gone." Tears formed in her eyes and shone in the darkness.

"We will save her, but maybe not today." Jessie wanted to rescue her, but he didn't know if it was possible. He didn't want to admit that it could be too late for Rosie. Maybe they would have to kill her to get rid of this spirit, but how? "For now, we have to get out of here."

The darkness lifted and a mist swirled around the door. Through it he could see Gail. She was frightened. Close to the door. For a moment, her eyes flicked to the escape route and he willed her to take it. Then she saw him and a smile lit up her face. Turning away from the door, she started walking toward him.

He wanted to scream at her to run, to go, but he couldn't open his mouth, couldn't form the words.

In between them was Rosie.

Gail didn't hesitate. She pulled the Holy water from her pocket and splashed it on the woman.

Rosie sneered and pulled back.

"I call on you, my chosen ones. My acolytes appear now and give me your strength." Rosie held one hand on the necklace, and with her right hand stretched out, making a fist, she challenged the air.

The darkness appeared again and swirled around her, forming and coalescing into silhouettes.

For long seconds, the mist twisted into three shapes and then snapped back into a mist. The shadow was fighting. Mary's face emerged from the darkness. Her mouth contorted into a scream, her eyes hollow and dark. Then the mist was back, more transparent.

"I invite the Forces of Darkness to bestow their infernal

might upon me. Open the Gates of Hell, give me your power and come forth to obey me, Old Hag – Matron, the one who controls you through all eternity."

So he had been right, she was the Old Hag. They knew the name she used. Jesse exalted in gaining that one piece of the puzzle. Could it help them? He didn't know, but it was something… it was a start.

Three figures appeared out of the darkness, all wearing long black cloaks, the hoods flat upon their backs. On the left was an old lady. Her birdlike features drawn down in anguish. Long gray hair framed her face and made her look so very fragile, but there was strength there too and resolve in her eyes. Thin eyebrows knitted together, lips were drawn into a thin line, jaw tensed, and thin, wizened fingers clenched into fists. She was fighting.

Next to her was a scruffy looking man with a scar over his right eye. There was a smug, satisfied smile on his face. Thick lips like twin slugs curled into a smile, and as he looked at Matron, adoration appeared on his face.

On the right was a bemused young man. Shoulder length, impossibly black hair flopped over his eyes. It gave him the look of a puppy trying to please its master. His face wore the expression of one who had imbibed too much and didn't quite know where he was. It said that, I *will wake up soon and joke about this night for a long time to come.*

Jesse knew that if these acolytes joined with Matron, they had lost. They would multiply her power and make it even harder to send her away. What could he do?

Closing his eyes, he focused his mind on the problem and waited for his instincts to kick in. *Trust your instincts and reach for your power*, was what Sylvia had told him. So he reached and tried to trust. Doubt was like a weight on his shoulders, but he shook it off and trusted.

The answer came to him. There would be an altar, somewhere she would have a place where she goes to connect with the underworld. If he can't get to the necklace, then maybe he could get to that. To the place where she recharged her darkness. If he could get rid of that, it would lessen her power over the spirits that she was controlling. If he could also remove her necklace, they would have a real chance.

So, not much to do.

At that thought, he felt a presence… just for the briefest of moments, his spirit guides had connected with him. He was left with the feeling of love and also laughter. The old man, the one of whose motives he was not sure, he always seemed to be laughing.

Knowing that he was not entirely alone gave him strength. "You know what to do!" he shouted at Gail and saw her nod her head.

She turned from him and began to chant. He knew that her exorcism would be from the heart. The words would be her own, but the feeling in delivery was what counted and she had the heart of an angel, the courage of a lion, and the strength of an elephant. She would do what needed to be done.

Matron stood, surrounded by her acolytes, her eyes closed as she built up her power. The battle was about to begin and he prayed they had the courage and the fortitude to see it through.

"If you get the chance, get out of here," he said to Amy. "This is going to be long, scary, and dangerous. I don't know if any of us will survive. If we don't make it out by morning, burn this house to the ground and never come back."

Amy's eyes widened and her mouth opened. It stayed there for a second or two and then she closed it and nodded.

CHAPTER 27

"*L*ORD, bless Gail, the righteous; surround her with Your favor as with a shield." Jesse moved toward the apparitions. His first instinct was to lend Gail some help while he circled around them to get to the stairs. Then he would try to free the spirits. For now they were tethered here by Matron, so if he could free them, maybe they would leave. The boy would probably hang around… he didn't understand where he was, what he was doing. Jesse could help him once the battle was over. For now freeing him would be enough. The man, even when free, would rally with Matron, and the woman, she looked frightened. Hopefully, at least she would go.

He recited an exorcism as he splashed them with Holy water, but it felt like an uphill struggle, a losing battle. The spirit was filling his mind with despair and he had to fight against it.

Gail was closest to Rosie. She held her Holy water in her right hand and stepped toward the woman trying, her hardest to remember the exorcism.

"God's Word is made flesh; I command you, be gone. Be gone, Satan, master of all deceit, the enemy of man. Unclean and evil beast, hear the Lord's words and be gone from this place. I command you, be gone." Gail splashed Rosie with her Holy water.

At first the spirit withered inside the woman. It was like a darkness falling from her, but it didn't go far and rose to the surface, darkening her features like blight as the water sizzled from her skin.

"Geoffrey, oh loyalist of my acolytes. I command thee, destroy this woman." Matron turned toward Gail and sneered.

Jesse ran between Gail and the spirit. He expected the man to pass straight through him. Expected to feel the bone-chilling cold as the ghost dematerialized inside him, but Geoffrey stopped.

Anger crossed the spirit's bitter face and he raised his arm as if to strike out.

"In the Name of Jesus, I rebuke the spirit of Geoffrey," Jesse said, turning toward the man and staring right into his eyes. He willed him to be gone, pouring all his power, all his hopes into the words he was using. "I command you, leave this place, without manifestation and without harm to me or anyone, so that He can dispose of you according to His Holy Will."

Matron roared and shot forward.

Geoffrey, spluttered and faded for a moment as if he had been powered down. But, then he was back.

Rosie lagged behind and streaked across the room, her body blurred as the spirit raced for Jesse. Rosie was snapped back, and when they struck him, they were both together. One force, one solid weapon, and it knocked him off his feet.

Matron never faltered, but kept going and ran for her knife. She snatched it from the floor. Then she turned to Amy, raising it above the woman's head, smiling as she began to plunge it down toward her throat.

Amy shrank back as fear widened her eyes and froze her to the spot.

Jesse sprawled on the floor, winded once more and too far away to do anything. Why had he let Amy come? He knew it was a recipe for disaster. He knew that it was dangerous and foolish, but he had been weak. He had let Gail persuade him. When would he learn to trust his own instincts?

The knife arched through the air.

Geoffrey looked on, glee glowing in his dark eyes.

Gail stepped toward Matron, but she was too far away. The knife was falling fast, so very fast.

A shadow formed behind Matron. It was just a smudge across the room. It was only then that Jesse realized the old woman had gone.

The shadow deepened until he could see a thin figure in a dark cloak: Mary. Would she help Matron? Would she lend her power to the Old Hag's? It didn't matter. Though he tried to move, tried to travel the distance, there wasn't time. Before he had crossed even halfway, the knife would fall and Amy would be dead.

Desolation washed over him, but he pushed through it and moved as fast as he could.

A pink blur came out of the cloaked figure and passed through Rosie.

The knife halted… it stopped in mid-air, just inches from Amy's face. They could see Rosie fighting, and the knife wavering.

"Amy, move!" Jesse yelled, and covered the ground between them. This time he pushed Rosie as hard as he could. Though it felt wrong to hit a woman so hard, he knew it was for the best.

She started to fall and he kicked her in the back. Gail was by his side.

"I cast you out, unclean spirit; in the name of our Lord, Jesus Christ, be gone from this place. Leave us alone, leave these creatures of God." Gail rushed to where Rosie had fallen and pried the knife from her hand.

They were winning. Jesse looked at Mary and nodded his thanks. The spirit was translucent, but she became a touch clearer and the smile she gave him was one of joy.

Rosie lay sprawled on the floor, her face a jumble of emotions. It looked like Rosie was fighting.

Gail held on to the knife, staring at it as if she didn't quite know what to do.

Jesse knew that it was now or never. They had a reprieve, but it wouldn't last. Matron was disorientated. He had to find the altar…had to destroy it, but if he left the room then he left Gail and Amy vulnerable to the power of the spirit.

Looking down at Rosie, he tried to see through her, to work out if she was beaten. There was nothing… no expression. That was a bad sign, but instinct told him to go now.

"Mary, where is her seat of power, her altar?"

Mary formed before him and opened her mouth. No words came out and she shook her head sadly. Then she pointed and started to move toward the stairs. Jesse understood. It would be in one of the bedrooms. If the house had a cellar it would have been there, but the spare room would be the next most logical place, somewhere quiet and out of the way.

"Can you show me?" he asked, knowing that the time it took for him to search the house could be too much. It could be the difference between victory and failure, between life and death.

Mary nodded and floated toward the stairs. She was weaker now, fading fast, but the smile on her face was genuine enough.

Jesse followed as quickly as he could. As he moved onto the stairs and when he lost sight of Gail, he so wanted to look back. To hesitate, to check out what was happening, but every instinct told him that time was of the essence.

Trust your instincts.

Taking the steps two at a time, he followed the ghost, watching as she became more and more translucent until she was just a mist before him.

"Mary!" Matron screamed from below. The voice was dark, guttural, and worthy of a Carlsberg advert.

Mary turned and pointed and there was anguish on her face. She mouthed something, probably hurry, and then she was gone.

Jesse understood that she had been jerked back into Matron. That meant that the spirit was back in control. She was strong and dangerous now. His foot poised on the top step. Should he turn and run down to save Gail, or should he continue upward and destroy the altar?

Trust your instincts.

It was the most difficult decision of his life and what was only a fraction of a second, seemed like forever. He wavered between running up and down, but in the end he knew there was only one choice.

If he went down, then Matron had won. If she could pull Mary back, then she was full of power. Too much for him to fight. He had to reduce that power and destroying her altar was the beginning.

Racing up the stairs, he called on his spirit guides: "Guide me, wise ones. Lead me to the place of the Old Hag's power. Let me help Gail, Amy, and Rosie. Be with me in the dark places and guide me back to the light."

Instantly he knew to turn right at the top of the stairs, and he raced past the first door all the way to the end of the corridor, to the very last door. He burst into the room. Would he be in time?

CHAPTER 28

Rosie/Matron lay sprawled on the floor. What had happened? It was unacceptable that she could be knocked down, and now Mary was leading her enemy away. Looking for her altar. It was unacceptable, such betrayal. If he got there and destroyed her seat of power, then she would be weakened... she might even fail.

For a moment she thought about running, just picking up this weak and useless body and leaving this place. Maybe she should go back to RedRise House. It had been safe there. She had been safe there. She could regroup and rest and then come out once more.

Inside her mind. Rosie laughed. "I knew you would give in," she taunted. "I knew you were weak and powerless. My friends will defeat you."

Matron screamed and rose to her feet. It was time to go, to leave this place and to flee back to safety. She hated to leave Geoffrey but he was all that kept her here. This had all been a mistake.

Then she felt Rosie relax and her real thoughts were revealed. The coward was trying to save her friends. She intended to take her back to RedRise and kill this body. Once again Matron would be trapped in that house. How many years would it be before she could find another vessel with which to escape?

Fury filled her with strength, and she closed her eyes. Summoning all her power, she sent pain into Rosie's mind and pushed her away. More and more pain she sent until Rosie pulled back so far that she could not even sense her presence. Maybe she was gone for good. That didn't matter. The pleasure she gained from taunting her could be transferred to Mary. With a grin on her face, she called on her, "Come to me, oh sacred blade and let me give you the blood you desire."

The knife, her athame, was still in Gail's hand. The doe-eyed woman looked down at it as it twitched in her fingers. It was laughable and infused Matron with power.

These fools had believed they could banish her, but they are weak, pathetic, and would make a wonderful addition to her dark harem of spirits.

"Come to me, blade of mine." The knife flew from Gail's hand and straight to her. Reaching out she clasped onto it and then began a satanic ritual to bind her spirits and build her power. "I invoke the four Crowned Princes of Hell."

Pointing the knife to the east: "Lucifer, give your power to mine."

Pointing the knife to the north: "Beelzebub, grace me with your energy."

To the west: "Astaroth, I worship you, bind these souls to me."

To the south: "Azazel, complete me with your power."

The air darkened and she called on Mary, demanding that the weak old woman return to her side.

It should have been easy. Rosie was gone, for now, hopefully for good. She had three spirits, three acolytes. They should instill her with power and yet, the only one to do so was Geoffrey.

"Mary!" she screamed into the air. The word reverberated around the room and up the stairs.

Nothing happened for seconds, and yet it seemed like forever to Matron. Every millisecond would bring Jesse closer to her altar. Closer to destroying her. If she got Mary back, she would be able to send a wave of destruction through this house. It would knock him off his feet and keep her power safe.

Straining, pulling, panting with the effort she gave it her all, for if she could not control this one weak spirit then it was over.

Would she fail in this simple task? Would this weak and timid creature beat her?

Jesse was at the top of the stairs, so close to her destruction.

No, never. With her right hand she held the knife; with her left, she grabbed onto the fabric of reality and pulled it to her, hauling Mary back by her very essence.

A scream rang in her mind. Was it Mary or Rosie? She couldn't tell but something broke. Something slick and wet inside wrenched free and the pressure eased. Power flooded

THE BATTLE WITHIN

through her, and Mary was coming back, adding her spirit, albeit reluctantly, to her base of power.

Mary streamed down the stairs to settle at her side, once more wearing the dark robe of an acolyte. The weak old woman had fought hard, but now she would do as Matron needed.

Matron turned her attention to James, the last of her acolytes. If she brought his will to hers then, she would be unbeatable.

Entering his mind, she showed him his death. Terror turned his legs to rubber, but she hauled him up as he threatened to fall. "You are eternal now, strong, and meaningful. Be with me and I can show you the world."

James turned to her. Tears formed in his eyes and images of family and friends flooded his mind. She was going to lose him. Then she picked on the image of a young girl, maybe seven or eight years of age, wearing a princess costume. "Join me, or this will happen."

Into his mind she sent a picture of the girl pulled apart like a broken doll. Tossed to the floor, her lifeless eyes stared up at him, accusingly.

James sobbed and it broke his mind. He retreated from the vision and swarmed to her side. The power was amazing and she was ready to take on the world.

MATRON RAISED HER ARMS, commanding a wind with them, it whirled around the room. Picking up paper, ornaments, and an old shoe. It tore pictures from the walls and circled them like debris caught in a hurricane, tossing and turning with the ferocity of the storm.

Gail and Amy were thrust to the sides of the room tossed aside like yesterday's garbage. The tempest she invoked would fill the house. Jesse could not withstand it, and soon he would be beaten and battered by the power of her will.

The noise and destruction rose to a crescendo of devastation until nothing in the room was still, except Matron. Like a demonic conductor, she orchestrated the melee with a smug smile on her face. Furniture joined in the squall… the faded pink sofa thundered around the room, joined by a matching chair, the television, and a cheap glass stand.

Centrifugal force crushed Gail against the wall nearest to the door. Amy was flung to the opposite wall.

Matron stood in the center of the room the knife in her right hand held like a baton. Surrounding her were the three spirits. Geoffrey's face shone with darkness, his eyes lit with awe. Mary's was blank, and the bemused expression on James's face had changed to one of horror.

She had won. With a sense of great satisfaction, she walked easily through the storm toward Amy.

The fear in the woman's eyes filled her with delight.

* * *

JESSE KNEW he was going in the right direction. A tug inside pulled him forward and he searched his feelings. Was this instinct or was he being guided? It didn't matter and there was no time to analyze it now.

He rushed into the room and was rewarded with his goal.

Across the room was a table with a black cloth on it. Behind the table, on the wall, a pentagram had been painted. It was at least 8 feet high and wide and looked as if it was scrawled in blood.

It pulled his eyes and filled his veins with ice water. Something about it made him feel cold, weak, and totally insignificant. The confidence that led him here was suddenly gone, replaced by doubt. It made him want to stop, to give in.

Shaking his head, he walked forward. The effort for each step was like the last half mile of a marathon he had once run. It was too much. His muscles screamed, begging him to just give in. Exhaustion hung heavily on him, but he pushed on. This was the spirits' enrapture. The altar was strong and was giving him these feelings of powerlessness. He must fight them.

One more step; just focus on one step at a time. He grabbed hold of the bracelet on his wrist and felt the fuzziness clear away. He could do this.

On each side of the table was a black candlestick, and in the middle was a large book. It was opened to what looked like a blank page.

As he started forward, blood red writing appeared on the page. He was too far away to read it, but he knew that it was the story of his failure. It would tell of his, Amy's, and Gail's deaths… of how their souls were added to Matron's power.

No! How could he let himself be used?

Then don't. The voice in his head was Sylvia's, and it spurred him on.

That page wasn't completed yet. And if it ever was, he would tear it out of that book and he would burn it and stamp on the ashes with every ounce of strength he had left.

Spurred on, he surged across the room. He was so close. He knew that Gail would be undergoing something similar. She may be fighting for her life… he had to shut out those thoughts. If he could break a line on the pentagram and pull off the altar cloth, then Matron's power would be reduced.

It was a small room. He was half-way there. All he had to do was take five more steps and he could rip off that cloth.

Dashing, running, one step, two, the room filled with a hurricane that picked him from his feet and pushed him back to the door. It knocked him through it and then slammed the door shut behind him.

The once quiet hallway was a tsunami of sound and wind. Pictures flew past him as he fought to hold his ground, to work his way back to the door. He was fighting both the wind and the urge to race down the stairs to help Gail.

Despair advanced toward him as the wind fought his limbs. He wouldn't make it; he couldn't make it.

A vase hurtled through the air, crashing into his head.

CHAPTER 29

Matron took the time to gloat, staring down at Amy as she shivered on the floor at her feet. The knife, her Athame, was strong, warm, and powerful in her hand. The handle, slick with blood, was like an old friend in her palm.

Holding it high above her head, she let the wind die down, let her guard drop as she savored this victory.

Once Amy was dead, all resistance inside would be gone. Rosie would be so broken, her mind shattered into a thousand fragile pieces of denial, despair, and what-ifs. Victory was sweet on her tongue, all her worries had been for nothing. How had she ever believed that these puny creatures were a threat to one as old and powerful as she?

With her acolytes now on her side. She waited for Amy's terror to grow, to rise to a crescendo. Amy's eyes were so wide, her mouth, a thin line quivered, and her limbs refused to move.

It was perfect.

The knife began its gentle arc through the air. In just moments it would connect with Amy's throat and would tear open her jugular, covering Matron with fresh hot blood.

She licked her lips in anticipation as the knife fell.

* * *

Pushed back against the wall, Gail could only watch in despair as Matron approached the other woman. The wind howled around her, pressing her against the wall with a force so hard it pushed her cheeks against her teeth and strained her neck.

"Be gone, foul beast!" she shouted, but the wind caught her words in the air and threw them back in her face. It was like whispering next to a jet engine. No one was going to hear; no one was going to take notice.

Jesse had followed Mary, he would be working to help them. All she had to do was apply pressure. Somewhere in the scramble, she had lost her Holy water, but she could repeat the exorcism in her mind. It was the thought of the words that counted. How many times had Jesse told her that?

As she began to will that the spirit be driven from this room, Mary appeared behind Matron. She was back in the black robes and she looked scared, beaten. Maybe it was over.

* * *

Rosie knew she was fading, losing. Matron was growing in strength at such a rate that she didn't know how much longer she could hold on. But she could watch, and she had seen the courage that Mary had shown. The woman wanted to help and she deserved help in return. Maybe helping her would help them all.

Digging deep inside, she wanted to scream as her body approached her best friend with the knife raised above her head. Would she have to watch as she killed Amy? It was almost too much to bear, but she tried to send a message to her friend, letting her eyes shine with love, not hate. *Hold on, my friend. I will try to help you,* she whispered in her mind before she pulled back inside her vault and concentrated on the releasing prayer she had found at RedRise House.

It had been in the books *The Sacrifices of RedRise House* and the *Resurrection of Old Hag,* and she had used it to free the spirits of some of the children. Maybe she could use it now to release Mary.

Searching her mind, she shut out the horror before her, shut out the sight of her friend, now very much afraid and in mortal danger. All she had time for was the words. Could she remember them? Almost straight away, they said in her mind as if they had been put there *In the Name of Jesus, I rebuke the spirit of Mary Price. I command you leave this place, without manifestation and without harm to me or anyone, so that He can dispose of you according to His Holy Will.*

When she had done this at the house, the children had smiled at her and then had faded out of existence. She didn't know where they went, but it felt good and right and she hoped that this act would release Mary and slow Matron down.

Her arm was starting to fall. The knife would be rushing toward Amy. It was too late; her friend was all but dead.

* * *

MARY FOUGHT against the Old Hag's hold, but it was too strong. She was bound to her, forced to watch in horror as another soul would be claimed. Then she felt a tug inside, a warmth to chase away the cold, and she heard Rosie's prayer.

It was like a chain was removed from her neck, as though her hands were suddenly freed from the shackles that bound her to the spirit. She could leave; she could be free. But she watched as Amy cowered back against the wall. This strong woman was so afraid that she was unable to move. Mary wanted to go to her, to help her, but it wasn't her place.

There was another tug, one that felt like love. She glanced behind her and saw a bright white light. It welcomed her and she wanted to go to it with every fiber of her soul. It called her home, but the thought of Amy's terror would not let her leave.

For a moment, she turned, but then she rushed forward, through the Old Hag. As she did, Matron shuddered. It knocked her off balance and the knife fell from her hands.

Mary turned to see Rosie beneath the façade of the Matron, and she smiled, nodding a thank you. The call of the light was overpowering now and she had no choice but to go with it. Matron was starting to stand. She was reaching for the knife, but so was Amy. Mary wanted to stay to help, but she couldn't resist the calm, the peace that called to her. As she passed the Old Hag. she reached out to clasp the necklace, the pentagram that hung around Rosie's neck. Instinctively she knew it was the woman's power, but she was already leaving this plane and her fingers passed right through the chain.

Peace washed over her as she was surrounded by light. There was a fleeting thought for those left behind, but soon even that was gone. Their journey was not hers and they would have to find their own way.

***

AS MARY SMILED, Rosie felt Matron's hold loosen, felt the knife fall from her fingers. Now she was fighting once more. Struggling to stop her limbs from moving. At the same time she could see Amy. Her friend was throwing herself forward, trying to reach the knife before she could. It would be touch and go. They were closer, but Matron would have to fight Rosie every inch of the way.

Amy reached for the knife at the same time as Gail came up behind Rosie. She pushed hard, knocking her away from the knife. Then she saw her bottle of Holy water. It had landed against the wall and was just a few feet away.

Amy was stiff reaching for the knife. She grabbed hold of it but, the desperate plunge had left her off balance and she rolled over and closer to Matron. Gail could hear a struggle start as she picked up the water.

Turning, she could see Matron beneath the skin of Rosie. It was as if a negative and positive image were laid one over the other. They were fighting an internal battle and Matron was struggling to get to Amy. The three-way fight continued while Gail took a breather. Jesse had told her that in situations like this, it was always quicker to step back, take stock and to let your instincts tell you what to do. She wanted to rush in, to shout, to scream, and to throw the rest of her Holy water over this evil witch, but she knew that it would have little effect.

She began to chant, putting her heart and soul into releasing Matron from this plane. As she did so, Geoffrey appeared before her. There was malice in his eyes. They burned and knocked her back with their fury.

For a moment, the two circled each other. Could he hurt her? She knew it was doubtful, from what she had learned. However, it seemed that with every case, the lines got redrawn as she learned a new trick or two.

Then it came to her… she tossed Holy water over Geoffrey and watched him coil back with revulsion.

"In the Name of Jesus," she repeated the words that she had heard in her head earlier, the words she knew had come from Rosie. As she got to the part of his name, she said the words without knowing what they would be. "I rebuke the spirit of Geoffrey Davis. I command you leave this place, without manifestation and without harm to me or anyone, so that He can dispose of you according to His Holy Will."

Geoffrey screamed and shrank in on himself. He was sucked back inside of his own body until there was nothing left but a dark spot. Once more, she threw Holy water over the darkness and it fizzled out of existence to the sound of an eternal scream of despair.

Ignoring everything, she rushed to help Amy. The battle was not going well.

CHAPTER 30

Jesse woke on the floor. There was a pain in his head and neck, but he jerked awake and up to his feet. "Gail!" he screamed into the wind, only to find that the wind had dropped, leaving the hallway littered with pictures and debris. What did that mean? Was it over? Had they lost?

It didn't matter; he would do what he came up here to do. He had to continue in the vein that there was still hope. Moving hurt his head, but he forced his battered and bruised body to rush. The door in front of him was closed, but he didn't hesitate. Taking a run, he charged at it with all the strength he had left.

His shoulder hit the weak wood and he turned the handle. The door gave much easier than he'd expected and he sprawled into the room.

The room looked exactly as it had when he had been forced from it, earlier – how much earlier he didn't know but he had to hope that it wasn't too long. "Hold on Gail," he shouted as he rushed toward the altar.

The closer he got, the more difficult it became. The air was thicker, pushing him backward toward the door. He dug in his heels and surged forward inch by painful inch. Now it was hard to breathe. His lungs were deflated with the pressure and he gasped as he struggled to bring precious air into his starved lungs.

He was so close. The fact that it was still a struggle gave him hope. If she was still defending this, then she still needed her power.

One step, two, three. He could almost reach the altar cloth and he stretched his hand out further when, below him, he heard an inhuman shriek. "Gail, Gail, hang on, my love."

Though his heart wanted him to turn and run to her, his mind and instincts told him the best way to help was to stretch forward just a few millimeters more and yank that black cloth off the table.

He stretched and pushed against the solid wall of air. Straining, muscles screaming, his fingers brushed the cloth. It was cold and it sent a shock up to his heart. Again, he wanted to pull away but, he took another step, just a few centimeters closer, it was all he needed. Reaching out, he clasped hold of the cloth and ignored the cold darkness that threatened to engulf him.

Instead of drawing away he clasped his fingers tightly and pulled the cloth off the table.

* * *

GAIL REPEATED the exorcism and the Lord's Prayer as she approached Matron. Rosie was fighting, and sometimes the face that struggled with the knife as she rolled on the floor with Amy was hers. Other times, it was the dark and evil visage of the spirit that possessed her.

"Leave this place!" Gail shouted, and she poured the rest of her Holy water over Matron.

It did very little. In fact the woman smirked up at her, but that satisfied and smug smile took her attention for a moment. It was all they needed. Amy nodded and grabbed the knife from her hand. Rosie surfaced. Her face was drawn back into a shriek of defiance, and Gail reached out.

Gail had seen Mary's look as the ghost had faded away, and now she understood. With a thank you to the departed woman, she reached out and grasped onto the necklace that hung around the Old Hag's neck.

The chain was cold, heavy and it didn't want to move. Gail gritted her teeth and tried to pull back. As she did the other two women understood. Amy punched Rosie hard, just as Rosie threw her weight backward, and Gail did the same. Rosie fell away in front of Gail, and she fell backward.

The wind dropped and the room was quiet as a church on a Monday morning.

For a moment, they all stood still, shocked that this had happened. But Gail could see that Matron was rallying. That she intended to fight back even now.

Amy punched her friend again and Rosie nodded as she fell over backward and landed on the floor with her eyes closed.

* * *

Upstairs, Jesse threw the altar cloth to the floor and picked up one of the heavy candle holders. They were metal with square bases. With that, he approached the pentagram and scratched a gap in the blood on the wall. As he made a way through one of the lines, a wave of electricity passed over the wall, and the room was now just a spare room in desperate need of a tidy.

Jesse tossed the candle holder away and sprinted for the stairs. He raced down them mumbling over and over, "Gail, be safe, Gail, be safe, Gail..." his words died as he came into the wrecked living room to see Amy and Gail tying Rosie's unconscious body to a radiator.

He pulled Gail into his arms and kissed her. As he found her lips, tears fell from his eyes and ran down his face. Soon they broke their salty kisses, but he didn't want to let her go.

"Are you okay?" he asked as he searched her face. She was dirty, covered in dust and a few bruises, but she looked fine.

Gail nodded. "I'm fine. Mary helped us as did Rosie."

"Oh I love you so much. Marry me," Jesse blurted out the words before he could stop himself. For months he had been planning on doing this properly, and now he just blurted it out. It felt right, and the look on her face told him she felt it too.

"I wondered if you were ever going to ask," she said, and kissed him again.

"Is that a yes?"

Gail flung herself into his arms. "Yes, of course it's a yes. I love you too, dummy."

Amy appeared behind them and they pulled her into their arms and all hugged. At last, Jesse pulled free.

"Now, let's free your friend," he said.

In the corner Matron was waking. She hissed and pulled against the ties that held her. "You will never beat me," she shrieked.

"I think we have," Amy said. "Let my friend go."

"Never; she will die with me."

Amy coiled back and looked at Jesse. "Is that possible?"

Jesse thought about lying, but he knew there was no point. "Yes, it is, but what would your friend want?"

Amy nodded. "You're right. She would die to take this thing with her. Save her if you can, but I know what she would want."

"Take my hand," Jesse said, and he held out both hands. One for Gail and one for Amy. "Think of nothing but sending this evil to hell and freeing your friend. We can do this and we will."

They nodded and approached Matron.

James was blinking in and out of existence to one side of her. Confusion and fear fought for control of his face.

Gail looked at him… Jesse nodded. Gail let go of Jesse's hand and walked toward the young man. "It's all right," she said. "It's time for you to go to a better place. To a place of peace and beauty. To the next phase of your journey. Do not be afraid. Let go and walk toward the light."

"Stay with me you worm," Matron shrieked.

"She cannot hurt you," Gail said, and she reached out to him. Though she could not touch him, she could give a sense of warmth, of comfort, and instinctively she knew to do this. "Listen to me, block out her voice and listen to me. You are no longer afraid. You have passed from this life and it is time to go to the next. Let go, move on to peace. See the light and be free."

A light appeared behind him and an expression of rapture came over his face. Gently he floated away from them and was swallowed by the light.

Then Matron was all alone with the ones who wanted her gone. She let out a shriek that started off defiant but turned into something weak and pitiful. It looked like she knew it was over.

The three linked hands again. Jesse and Amy began to repeat the Lord's Prayer while Jesse chanted in Latin. Matron thrashed and writhed against the radiator.

"Pater noster, qui es in caelis, sanctificetur nomen tuum. Adveniat regnum tuum."

Rosie bucked inside her own body, fighting to push the spirit from her. She was praying that all would be well, but also knew this would be the start of her battle.

"Our Father, who art in Heaven, hallowed be Thy name. Thy kingdom come," Gail and Amy spoke together.

"Fiat voluntas tua, sicut in caelo et in terra." Jesse walked them closer to the writhing figure as she cursed and hissed and spat, her body shaking.

"Our Father, who art in Heaven, hallowed be Thy name. Thy kingdom come."

"You will pay for this, you will rot in hell." Matron spat the words and wrenched her hands free.

Jesse walked closer and they all kept repeating the exorcism. "Panem nostrum quotidianum da nobis hodie."

"Thy will be done on earth as it is in Heaven." Amy pulled back as Matron tried to stand, but Gail was having none of it. She reached out with her foot and putting it on Rosie's shoulder, she pushed the girl down.

"Et dimitte nobis debita nostra sicut et nos dimittimus debitoribus nostris."

Rosie was smiling now. Her features were taking control and the dark and evil visage that was Matron was fading.

"Give us this day our daily bread and forgive us our trespasses as we forgive those who trespass against us."

Rosie fell back and seemed to shrink. It was as if she had been blown up by the presence of the spirit.

"Et ne nos inducas in tentationem, sed libera nos a malo. Amen."

"And lead us not into temptation, but deliver us from evil. Amen."

As it passed from her, her clothes filled with air for a moment, and then she was alone. The sound of a scream echoed through the house. Matron was falling further and further down as she was dragged back to where she belonged.

It was over.

The friends collapsed into a heap on the floor, exhaustion, and hyper-emotion having taken their toll. It would be a

while before any of them would believe what had happened.
A while before their minds could face it.

EPILOGUE

Rosie sat in court waiting for the verdict to be read out. She was still thin and dark lines marred her eyes, showing that sleep was not easy to come by.

All the time she was possessed, she had tried not to eat and now she was finding food hard to stomach. Maybe she was punishing herself. That was what Amy told her, but every time she tried to eat, she thought of the spirits, the people she had killed.

She knew how lucky she was and she understood that she would have to take this punishment. Luckily, Amy, Gail, and Jesse had gotten her the best lawyer. Paul Simmons believed in the paranormal and understood what had happened. He was a good friend of Jesse and Gail and he had done everything he could to help Rosie.

Though he couldn't use ghost possession as a defense, he had muddied the water. He told the jury that Rosie had been subject to a terrible ordeal. She had been forced by an older, more forceful personality to commit the crimes, and she hadn't been alone when she committed them. The damage at the house, some inconclusive DNA results, and the injuries to Amy and Rosie had been enough to bring doubt. The police were not convinced, but they did concede that Rosie had an abusive boyfriend and that she had been badly beaten and scarred for life.

Paul hoped that it would be enough to get the jury to convict of manslaughter on the grounds of diminished responsibility. That way, Rosie would get time in a mental institute. It would be easier than prison, and she would have the possibility of parole.

Amy reached out and squeezed her shoulder as the jury came back in.

The judge had already given his direction. Though he hadn't told them what to do, he had offered Rosie some sympathy.

Once the jury had all filed into the court and sat down, the clerk of the court stood before them. Rosie didn't know what to feel. Her hands had killed, and yet she was a victim. She was happy to accept whatever happened to see the world freed of the evil Old Hag. That was what she had to remember.

The clerk of the court was speaking. "Will the jury please rise. Will the defendant also please rise and face the jury."

Rosie heard the scrape of chairs and she tried to stand, but her legs wouldn't hold her. Paul put his hand under her elbow and helped her to her feet.

"Mr. Foreman, has your jury agreed upon your verdicts?"

A kindly man of about fifty who looked like he was an accountant avoided her eyes as he spoke. "We have."

THE BATTLE WITHIN

"What say you Mr. Forman, as to complaint number 5879643, wherein the defendant is charged with three counts of first-degree murder? Is she guilty or not guilty?"

Rosie held her breathe as she heard a collective gasp behind her, and knew that Amy, Gail, and Jesse would all be wishing the verdict in her favor.

The Foreman turned toward her and Rosie felt her knees go weak. He looked down as if he couldn't face giving her such bad news.

"Not guilty."

Rosie let out a gasp and the court murmured and muttered. Rosie understood that the relatives would not be happy with this verdict and she felt for them. She wished that she could explain, but Jesse had told her that to do so would only make things worse. She had thought about writing a book, after all she was a writer.

"Order," the judge called.

Rosie knew the next charge had to be guilty, that she would serve a good part of her life in an institution, but still it felt like all her dreams had come true.

"What say you Mr. Forman, as to complaint number 5879644, wherein the defendant is charged with three counts of manslaughter on the grounds of diminished responsibility? Is she guilty or not guilty?"

"Guilty."

Rosie sunk down into her seat. She didn't hear anymore. Soon she felt Amy pull her into her arms. It was safe and comfortable and it may be the last time she would ever feel it.

"I'll visit you every week, I promise," Amy said. "Don't give up."

Rosie hugged her tight. "Thank you for saving me, for saving countless people. I don't care about this prison or where I go—it will be much nicer than being a prisoner in my own mind. Thank you Amy."

Guards came to take her away. As they guided her from the court, Rosie turned back.

"Thank you," she said, and this time she was talking to Gail and Jesse.

Once the doors had closed and the court had cleared, Paul turned to the three friends. "Don't despair. I will keep working. I will make sure she gets nice accommodations and that she is released as soon as possible. Most of all know, that your friend is free."

He stood and left the courtroom.

"What happened to him?" Amy asked.

"His wife was possessed. He managed to get her back, but her mind was never right again. She killed two people but she was lucky. There was no evidence. Trust him. Rosie will be fine and we will get her out in as few years as possible."

"I do," Amy said. "I know Rosie, she is stronger than she knows. She will survive this. Now, I have just one more question."

Jesse cocked his head and waited.

"What is it?" Gail asked as she reached out and took Amy's hands. "Whatever it is we will do our best for you."

"I just wondered if I would be invited to the wedding."

Gail laughed and pulled her into her arms, grabbing hold of Jesse she pulled him into the hug. As they pulled apart she smiled.

"Invited, how would you like to be my maid of honor?"

Amy nodded and wiped tears from her eyes. "I would like that."

* * *

IF YOU MISSED the first book in this amazing series The Ghosts of RedRise House The Sacrifice get it now http://a-fwd.to/7APCHD3

To find out when book three is available join my newsletter now **http://eepurl.com/cGdNvX**

CALLED FROM BEYOND – PREVIEW

6th July, 2018

Country Road,

Yorkshire

England

11:59 p.m.

Mark stared out through the windscreen at the dark and twisty road ahead. The long drive back to civilization dulled his senses and the warm car tempted him with sleep. He stifled a yawn and shook his head to fight the fatigue. "We probably should have stayed the night." Taking his eyes off the road, he turned to face Alissa.

Her feet were curled up on the seat next to her, her eyes almost closed. "Mmm, probably. It was good to see them again," she said, pushing her long blonde hair back from her face.

He loved to see it when it fell in whispers across her pale skin, so fine and silky to the touch. Right now, he just wanted them back in the hotel so he could hold her. These bleak and lonely roads were no place for a couple of city kids like them, and he couldn't wait to get back to the noise and bustle of Leeds.

They had booked a room at a hotel in one of the small villages—he had hoped to make it a bit of a romantic night as well as a reunion—but now he wished they hadn't. Maybe he should have taken her away somewhere special, not just down the road from their house?

"It *was* good," he said, pulling his eyes back to the road. "They both looked so healthy. And the food? Mmmm. Amazing."

"Don't I know it." Alissa's bright smile contrasted with the dreamy quality her eyes still held. "That stroganoff was so creamy and delicious. I think that's why I'm so sleepy. I'm way too full."

Mark laughed. "Or perhaps a few too many glasses of red wine?"

"You're jealous because tonight was your turn to drive." She stuck her tongue out and her green eyes danced with laughter.

"Funny, that." He tried to put a stern expression on his face. "It's always your turn to drive on the way there and mine to drive back."

"Yeah, I like the way that works out." She snorted a giggle and closed her eyes again. "Perfect, if you ask me."

Mark laughed and turned back to the road. Fatigue was like a heavy blanket and his eyes just wanted to close. He quickly rubbed a hand through his short brown hair. Though he was no longer enlisted, he never let his hair grow more than a finger. He unwound the window and let a cool breeze travel across his scalp. The fresh draft was much more invigorating than the cold air from the blowers. Right now, he needed something to bring back his concentration. At least another twelve miles laid between them and anything that even remotely resembled an A road.

"Do you think they made the right decision?" Alissa asked.

"You mean moving out here?"

"Yeah, it's a long way from London."

Mark thought about it. He missed their friends so he wanted to say no, then he thought about how much they'd laughed and smiled tonight. "We made the move for your job, what was it... three years ago now?"

"We moved to a city."

"Leeds is a big city but it's not London and you adapted."

Alissa grumbled. "I know, but right out in the country and into that old rundown house?"

"It looked pretty nice to me. They're happy there and that's all that counts, right?" It hit him hard that he wanted things to change. That she wanted more from the relationship was no secret and finally, he understood. He turned to look at her.

That pretty smile he loved so much mocked him just a little. She was a picture to behold with perfect skin, a heart-shaped face, and the biggest green eyes you ever did see. A splattering of freckles danced across her nose and more tiptoed down her arms.

Sometimes he tried to count them when she was asleep.

They had been engaged for a year now, but when he proposed, it had simply been a stop gap for him—a way to appease her—and he never intended the engagement as a prelude to marriage. That stank!

She gave everything to him, was always generous and loving. His best friend.

How could he treat her like that? He wanted to marry her, but this was the wrong time to set the date. He had to make it more romantic.

She deserved that.

"Keep your eyes on the road," she gently admonished.

Nodding, he turned back. The headlights hardly cut through the gloom and he eased up on the accelerator, slowing the car just a touch. The beams of light shone into the ether as they topped a brow, and then dropped to the tarmac as they began to descend. The dark and twisted trees lining the road on their right sucked the light from the moon. To their left, the ground sloped alarmingly away and more trees, along with the occasional sheep, dotted the grassland. He hated the fact that sheep were on the road. Where were the fences? Surely farm animals were supposed to be fenced in for safety?

"Penny for them?" she said, bringing him back to the moment and the feelings that had snuck up on him.

"Why don't we stay another night? We could come for a walk on the moors, have a nice romantic meal, and then just chill a little."

Alissa laughed, a silky sound that stroked down his nerves and filled him with love. "When I look out the window all I can hear is, *Stay on the road—keep clear of the moors.*"

Mark laughed. What other woman would get his favorite film? An old one, for sure, but still the best. "Maybe we could find a pub called the Slaughtered Lamb?"

Alissa chuckled. "No, that would be too freaky."

Green eyes opened wide, staring, as her mouth dropped open.

"Mark!" her voice was high pitched and cut through the joy like a knife through silk.

The world slowed as he turned his head back to the road.

The headlights barely penetrated the soft mist in front of them, but he clearly saw a woman standing there. A white dress fluttered around her thin frame. Her face seemed carved in granite.

Frozen in an eternal scream.

Mark yanked on the steering wheel and jerked the car to the left. He tensed, waiting for the crunch as steel hit flesh and broke bones—a sound he knew well—and a memory of war flashed into his mind. Broken flesh. Blood. A world of fear and pain.

Pulling himself from the nightmare of his past, he yanked harder on the wheel and trusted his reactions were good. The car turned instantly. The force pushed him into the seat but it shouldn't have been quick enough to miss the woman. He tensed for the crunch but it never came, just a flutter of white whipped across the windscreen.

They left the road and tore across the grass. Like a turbo powered shopping trolley, they careered down the hill, out of control.

Trees loomed out of the black as the headlights and power

went out. The car plunged into darkness. The engine had died but, nevertheless, they hurtled on down the hill. Mark pulled left and right, avoiding a sheep then a tree. Everything lurched out of the dark and was on them so soon. His right foot pressed hard on the brakes, but nothing happened. Stamping his foot down on the clutch, he pushed the gear lever into first. The car should have slowed considerably, had to slow, but it didn't. Before he could do anything else, another tree loomed out of the darkness and engulfed them.

This time, the crunch was bone wrenching as they ground to a halt. He instinctively reached out to his left to steady Alissa, but was too late. They both flew forward until they hit their seatbelts.

Another crunch and breaking glass showered him as the car finally shuddered to a halt.

In the pitch black, Mark's ears rang and his chest hurt. His training kicked in and he assessed the situation and his own injuries. Nothing but cuts and bruises. His neck was jarred and his knees had impacted with the steering column. They ached like hell, but the seat belt had saved him from worse injuries.

The car was stable for now, but how was Alissa? Leaves cut out the moon and he could only make out shapes. As his eyes adjusted to the dark, he searched for her and his phone. The seat belt was in the way. He couldn't reach the clasp. Fighting down terror, he methodically searched for the catch.

Alissa! The thought of her injured threatened to drive him to panic, but that wouldn't help. Although his chest ached from the seatbelt strain, he managed to cough out, "Babe, are you okay?" So far, he couldn't hear her moving but it could just be that the compression from the bang had affected his ears.

Many a shell blast had given him a permanent ringing, but now they were almost screaming at him. Why was it so dark? Why had the lights gone out? He didn't know but they had no time to worry about that now. They had to get out of the car.

At last, he managed to free the seat belt and tipped forward. Reaching for his phone, he pulled it from his pocket and shook it twice. The torch light lit up and he almost let out a wail of grief.

Alissa was looking at him. Her eyes were glassy. Not the glassy darkness of death. This was the shine of shock, of trauma. He had to act quickly.

"Hey, baby, how are you?" He spoke gently but as matter of factly as he could.

Her eyelashes fluttered. She was awake and aware. That was good. For a moment, the woman on the road came to mind, but he pushed the thought away. They had missed her, but it didn't matter. Even if he had hit her, he could do nothing about it now. *Deal with what you can.* That was what his training had taught him. *Don't go looking for more trouble.* Once he had gotten Alissa out of danger, he would search for the woman.

He checked Alissa for injuries and a groan nearly escaped him as panic threatened to overwhelm.

She was leaning back against the seat. Her face looked fine, just pale, but that wasn't what scared him so.

A tree branch jutted out of her left shoulder. The gnarled and green wood had pierced straight through her light green top, through flesh, blood, and sinew, and into the car seat.

Think!

For a moment, he grasped the branch sticking out from her shoulder.

Alissa let out a groan of anguish and he pulled his hand away.

Blood was leaking from the wound, just a trickle. If he pulled the branch clear, he would be able to move her from the car but the wound would bleed much more quickly. If she had severed an artery, she would be dead before he could do anything to stop it.

First aid kit!

He sprang from the car and battled the branches of an oak tree. They crumbled easily with each strike. The old and weary tree could topple onto the car any second now. Alissa would be crushed. Each groan and creak of the limbs surrounding him forced a bead of sweat onto his forehead.

He pulled up the coordinates of where they were on his phone, then dialed for an ambulance as he moved around to the back of the car.

Mark popped the boot and immediately spotted the first aid kit strapped against the wheel arch.

"Emergency services, which service please?"

"Ambulance," he said as he grabbed the kit. Alissa's door was buried deep beneath unstable branches. He didn't want to waste time digging her out or risk disturbing the hovering tree, so he went back to the driver's side.

With the phone clamped between his neck and shoulder, he opened the kit and crawled back into the car.

What now!?

"Help me?" Alissa pleaded. On her cheeks, the glint of tears mocked his indecisiveness.

"I'm here, baby. You'll be out of here any minute."

"Ambulance, what's your emergency?"

Mark explained as he packed around the wound with gauze.

"The ambulance is on the way. You need to leave her where she is and go back to the road to help guide the driver to the right spot," the operator told him.

Mark recognized the tone, designed to keep him calm and busy. For a moment, he thought about it. But he couldn't leave her. The tree groaned above him, how long would it hold? Would he get her out before it came crashing down?

Alissa's breathing was ragged now. Panicked.

Hearing her in such pain tore out his heart.

"I can't leave her and I have military training. Just get to these coordinates," he said and dropped the phone back into his pocket.

"You have to get me out of here." Alissa grabbed hold of his hand.

Her grip was weak, her fingers cold.

"I will, baby, but you must be patient."

Leaves rustled overhead and a branch fell, bouncing off the top of the car. They were out of time. He needed to get her out of there, but he'd have to pull the branch from her shoulder to do so. The angle was wrong from the driver's seat. If he did it from here, he would tear open her wound. If he did that, he doubted he'd be able to stop the bleeding in time.

She'd bleed out in his arms.

If he could get in through the passenger door, then it would be a cleaner jerk. The branch would come out at the same angle as it had entered her shoulder and he could staunch the flow more easily. If he could get her from the car, he could possibly even tie off the artery.

"Just hold still a moment," he said and pulled her fingers from his.

Panic gave her strength. Despite her small size, she clung on so desperately that he struggled to free his hand.

"I will just be a moment," he whispered against her ear, then gently kissed her hair. The blonde tresses were no longer silky but wet with blood. Had she hurt her head?

He couldn't worry about it now, so he left the car and fought his way to the front and through the fallen tree. A large branch was wedged against the door, and he kicked at it to break it free. The tree above them shuddered and rained down sticks and smaller branches. Something groaned and cracked, and still the door was wedged tight. He kicked at the branch with all his might, knowing he had a choice between time and force. Too much time and the tree might collapse on top of them, too much force and he might hasten that outcome. His foot hit the branch and it slid across the door. The tortured metal screamed but the branch fell away.

He pulled on her door, but the impact had bent the metal. His breathing was ragged, and the fear inside him fought like a wild horse for freedom but he reined it in. Feeling around the door, he found the dent and then kicked the panel to clear the frame.

Alissa let out a scream of pain.

Mark felt as if he had been stabbed in the gut, but he had to keep going. Grasping hold of the door, he pulled with all he had. For a moment, nothing happened and his muscles protested at the effort. Gradually, his eyes adjusted to the darkness as he worked to free the door.

With one last gargantuan effort, he hauled the door open as far as it would go.

Alissa's eyes were drawn down, her mouth grimacing in pain. That was a good sign. If she could feel, then she hadn't gone into shock yet and there was hope.

He fought around the door. Before he could lean into the car, a ripping sound dragged his gaze upward. A thick branch tore free from the trunk and fell down, and down. The massive limb smashed through the windscreen and slammed into Alissa's face with a dull thunk.

As warm wet splashed his face, Mark screamed, certain he'd never be able to stop.

* * *

Find out what mistakes Mark makes by reading Called From Beyond A Woman in White Ghost Story FREE on Kindle Unlimited http://a-fwd.to/1w2qbGw

THE HAUNTING OF SEAFIELD HOUSE – PREVIEW.

30th June 1901

Seafield House.

Barton Flats,

Yorkshire.

England.

1. am.

Jenny Thornton sucked in a tortured breath and hunkered down behind the curtains. The coarse material seemed to stick to her face, to cling there as if holding her down. Fighting back the thought and the panic it engendered she crouched even lower and tried to stop the shaking of her knees, to still the panting of her breath. It was imperative that she did not breathe too loudly, that she kept quiet and still. If she was to survive with just a beating, then she knew she must hide. Tonight he was worse than she had ever seen him before. Somehow, tonight was different, she could feel it in the air.

Footsteps approached on the landing. They were easy to hear through the door and seemed to mock her as they approached. Each step was like another punch to her stomach, and she could feel them reverberating through her bruises. Why had she not fled the house?

As if in answer, lightening flashed across the sky and lit up the sparsely furnished room. There was nothing between her and the door. A dresser to her right provided no shelter for an adult yet her eyes were drawn to the door on its front. It did not move but stood slightly ajar. Inside, her precious Alice would keep quiet. They had played this game before, and the child knew that she must never come out when Daddy was angry. When he was shouting. Would it be enough to keep her safe? Why had Jenny chosen this room? Before she could think, thunder boomed across the sky and she let out a yelp.

Tears were running down her face, had he heard her? It seemed unlikely that he could hear such a noise over the thunder and yet the footsteps had stopped. *Oh my, he was coming back.* Jenny tried to make herself smaller and to shrink into the thick velvet curtains, but there was nowhere else to go.

If only she had listened to her father, if only she had told him about Alice. For a moment, all was quiet, she could hear the house creak and settle as the storm raged outside. The fire would have burned low, and soon the house would be cold. This was the least of her problems. Maybe she should leave the room and lead Abe away from their daughter. Maybe it was her best choice. Their best choice.

Lightning flashed across the sky and filled the room with shadows. Jenny let out a scream for he was already there. A face like an overstuffed turkey loomed out of the darkness, and a hand grabbed onto her dress. Jenny was hauled off her feet and thrown across the room. Her neck hit the top of the dresser, and she slumped to the floor next to the door. How she wanted to warn Alice to stay quiet, to stay inside but she could not make a sound. There was no pain, no feeling and yet she knew that she was broken. Something had snapped when she hit the cabinet, and somehow she knew it could never be fixed. That it was over for her. In her mind, she prayed that her daughter, the child who had become her daughter, would be safe just before a distended hand reached out and grabbed her around the neck. There was no feeling just a strange burning in her lungs. The fact that she did not fight seemed to make him angrier and she was picked up and thrown again.

As she hit the window, she heard the glass shatter, but she did not feel the impact. Did not feel anything. Suddenly, the realization hit her and she wanted to scream, to wail out the injustice of it but her mouth would not move. Then he was bending over her.

"Beg for your life, woman," Abe Thornton shouted and sprayed her with spittle.

Jenny tried to open her mouth, not to beg for her own life but to beg for that of her daughter's. She wanted to ask him to tell others about the child they had always kept a secret, the one that he had denied. To admit that they had a daughter and maybe to let the child go to her grandparents. Only her mouth would not move, and no sound came from her throat.

She could see the red fury in his eyes, could feel the pressure building up inside of him and yet she could not even blink in defense. This was it, the end, and for a moment, she welcomed the release. Then she thought of Alice, alone in that cupboard for so long. Now, who would visit her, who would look after her? There was no one, and she knew she could never leave her child.

Abe grabbed her by the front of her dress and lifted her high above his head. The anger was like a living beast inside him, and he shook her like she was nothing but a rag doll. Then with a scream of rage, he threw her. This time she saw the curtains flick against her face and then there was nothing but air.

The night was dark, rain streamed down, and she fell with it. Alongside it she fell, tumbling down into the darkness. In her mind she wheeled her arms, in her mind she screamed out the injustice, but she never moved, never made a sound.

Instead, she just plummeted toward the earth.

Lightning flashed just before she hit the ground. It lit up the jagged rocks at the base of the house, lit up the fate that awaited her and then it was dark. Jenny was overwhelmed with fear and panic, but there was no time to react, even if she could. Jenny smashed into the rocks with a hard thump and then a squelch, but she did not feel a thing.

"Alice, I will come back for you," she said in her mind. Then it was dark, it was cold, and there was nothing.

Read <u>The Haunting of Seafield House</u> now just 0.99 or FREE on Kindle Unlimited.

MORE BOOKS FROM CAROLINE CLARK

Get a FREE short story and never miss a book. Subscribe to Caroline Clark's newsletter for new release announcements and occasional free content:
http://eepurl.com/cGdNvX

*   *   *

All Books are FREE on Kindle Unlimited

The Haunting of Seafield House **Gail wants to create some memories – if she survives the night in Seafield House it is something she will never forget.** http://a-fwd.to/6UXsowk

Called From Beyond – The Spirit Guide - **A Woman in White Ghost Story. A non-believer, a terrible accident, a stupid mistake. Is Mark going mad or was his girlfriend Called from Beyond?** http://a-fwd.to/1w2qbGw

DarkMan **The Haunting of Oldfield Drive. Alone in the dark, Margie must face unimaginable terror.**

Is this thing that haunts her nights a ghost or is it something worse? http://a-fwd.to/1U2C5gI

The Haunting of Brynlee House Based on a real haunted house - Brynlee House has a past, a secret, it is one that would be best left buried. http://a-fwd.to/2UiiG7w

The Haunting of Shadow Hill House A move for a better future becomes a race against the past. Something dark lurks in Shadow Hill House and it is waiting. http://a-fwd.to/5HMB7UX

The Ghosts of RedRise House – The Sacrifice Dark things happened in RedRise House. Acts so bad they left a stain on the soul of the building. Now something is lurking there... waiting... dare you enter this most haunted house? http://a-fwd.to/7APCHD3

Want Books for FREE before they hit Amazon?

Would like to become part of Caroline's advanced reader team?

We are looking for a few select people who love Caroline's books.

If accepted will receive a free copy of each book before it is released.

We will ask that you share the book on your social media once it is released and give us any feedback on the book.

You will also get the chance to interact with Caroline and make suggestions for improvements to books as well as for future books.

This is an exciting opportunity for anyone who love's the author's work. Click here to find out more details

Find all my books here:

USA http://amzn.to/2yYL9Pz

UK http://amzn.to/2z0W1MH

ABOUT THE AUTHOR

Want Books for FREE before they hit Amazon?

Would like to become part of Caroline's advanced reader team?

We are looking for a few select people who love Caroline's books.

If accepted will receive a free copy of each book before it is released.

We will ask that you share the book on your social media once it is released and give us any feedback on the book.

You will also get the chance to interact with Caroline and make suggestions for improvements to books as well as for future books.

This is an exciting opportunity for anyone who love's the author's work. Click here to find out more details.

Caroline Clark is a British author who has always loved the macabre, the spooky, and anything that goes bump in the night.

She was brought up on stories from James Herbert, Shaun

Hutson, Stephen King and more recently Darcy Coates, and Ron Ripley. Even at school she was always living in her stories and was often asked to read them out in front of the class, though her teachers did not always appreciate her more sinister tales.

Now she spends her time researching haunted houses or imagining what must go on inside them. These tales then get written up and become her books.

Caroline is married and lives in Yorkshire with her husband and their three boxer dogs. Of course one of them is called Spooky.

You can contact Caroline via her facebook page: https://www.facebook.com/CarolineClarkAuthor/

Via her newsletter: http://eepurl.com/cGdNvX

Or her website http://CazClark.com

She loves to hear from her readers.

SPOOKY
NIGHT BOOKS

I am also a member of the haunted house collective.
Why not discover great new authors like me?
Enter your email address to get weekly newsletters of hot new haunted house books:
http://.hauntedhousebooks.info

http://eepurl.com/cGdNvX
www.cazclark.com

Copyright © 2018 by Caroline Clark
All rights reserved.
No part of this book may be reproduced in any form or by any electronic or mechanical means, including information storage and retrieval systems, without written permission from the author, except for the use of brief quotations in a book review.
License Notes
This e-Book is licensed for personal enjoyment only. It may not be resold or given away to others. If you wish to share this book, please purchase an additional copy. If you are reading this book and it was not purchased then, you should purchase your own copy. Your continued respect for author's rights is appreciated.

This story is a work of fiction any resemblance to people is purely coincidence. All places, names, events, businesses, etc. are used in a fictional manner. All characters are from the imagination of the author.

Cover By www.dreamstonepublishing.com

Cover photo http://www.flickr.com/photos/37382793@N08/4086695693/'

Edited by Sandy Link

Printed in Great Britain
by Amazon